MYSTERY OF A NIGHTMARE

MYSTERY OF A NIGHTMARE

MOHNISH S. DESHPANDE

PARTRIDGE

To order additional copies of this book, contact
Partridge India
000 800 10062 62
orders.india@partridgepublishing.com

www.partridgepublishing.com/india

Acknowledgements

First and foremost, I would like to thank Partridge Publishing Company for providing this great opportunity to bring my work into the spotlight. Without their support, my manuscript would never come out of the cupboard.

I would like to thank my parents, who have always supported and motivated me to write more stories.

Special Thanks: Ambarish Deshpande, Rohan Mahajan & Manjusha Mahajan.

Thanks To My Wife, Manasi: My wife and I own a trading company. I would like to thank Manasi for supporting me, handling my office, and taking care of the entire business in my absence.

Dedicated To Sudhakar Mahajan: I want to dedicate this novel to my beloved father-in –law, who passed in February 2013.

CHAPTER 1

Nightmares have often scared many among us, and this blind girl had an incredible sense to look into the future or the past. The mystery began with a terrible dream.

The town looked like any other European urban area; maybe its name does not exist today, but once they called it Blitzland. During the years 1905-1910, people lived in two-story or three-story dusty houses, and since it was midnight, their colours couldn't be seen prominently. They lived here united but fear accompanied them more than their friends.

What did they fear?

The ghosts and the sorcerers!

Blitzland comprised forests, lake, palace, and many castles among which a few were abandoned.

Tonight, the town seemed to be wrecked in a ferocious battle between wise and imprudent. The houses were on fire, and souls of dead were burning in flames of revenge. The screams of townies shattered the peace of the night when enemies battered them mercilessly. Some of them were razed with fathomless haemorrhage and perished instantly. It all seemed like an epic war without imparting any justification for its cause. The defenders drew out the possibility that the antagonists might have meticulously executed evil's command since many of them worshipped evil to acquire powers and possessions. Their acquisitiveness turned rampant, and none of the properties satisfied them.

Followers of evil were the people who efficiently performed depraved rituals, including human sacrifice and naked blood-bath. Their greediness like the waxing moon grew to inspire them to rob and slaughter the townies and shed the blood as a tender tribute to the evil. The blood was streaming through the streets, proving to *the God of evil* that they have done immeasurable ferocious murders, and they believed that evil would give them what they desired.

Loretta Costigan, a charming adolescent, holding her attractive Edwardian dress above her ankles ran barefoot through a narrow lane. She was the only one to survive the attack without acute lacerations. She was fair-skinned; her hair bound in a bow, and her eyes were dark emerald; alluring but terrorised after having perceived the deadly war. The tiny stones on the streets have bruised her feet, but that pain was incomparable to what others were enduring. A few people wrapped in the flames ran on the street with their hands in the air. They were screaming as if thousands of knives ran through their skin at a time. Loretta had never seen anything like this before;

people on flames alive! She looked minutely through a slight crease between the houses and gazed upon a few kids who were frozen with fear; some cried while others stood with their eyes fixed at the horrifying scene: the enemies frightening and murdering people with flintlock rifles.

Loretta Costigan scampered through the winding path in the dense woods. Being swallowed by the growing mist, she halted on the lonely street; gasping and sweating. As she suspiciously trod further, the mist faded away revealing a massive gate of the garden that was meant for lovers. The entrance of garden had its name painted on a curved log: Morgane's Park.

Tonight, there were no lovers, no families, but a mother along with a baby knelt in front of two formidable enemies. She was begging for her life.

Despite the swelling effulgence of rising moon, Loretta barely saw their faces while she stood motionless, witnessing a heinous crime being committed.

'I beg your kindness. Please don't shoot me, I have a child,' the mother said, glancing at them anxiously with drenched eyes. She thought at least those monsters would show humanity and leave her, but the situation turned worse beyond imagination.

'I won't shoot if you admit to being my servant for rest of your life,' a soldier said.

'No, that is impossible. Please let me go,' the woman replied.

Why would she become their servant? She was an adorable lady, a caring mother, and a loving wife.

And what would the attackers benefit from taking her life?

Nothing.

However, politics dwelled in using the life, emotions, and religion of the people for ultimate political benefit and self-worth. Or why would have wars taken place in the world?

The woman's eyes appeared in tears; even so, filled with fear and anger at the same time. The gunmen were monsters with no mercy in their heart. They raised their weapon and shot her dead.

Now, Loretta witnessed this brutal murder and sprinted towards a chariot. She intended to ride out of the town, but the horses stopped on the crossroad and whinnied continuously. The sudden change in their behaviour annoyed Loretta. Several moments later, she came to know why the horses were refusing to proceed.

People believed that the animals such as dogs and horses have an extra sense due to which they can perceive the things those were invisible to human eyes. They could probably see the ghost!

Loretta stood almost paralysed for a few moments after realising that her assumption was correct. Emerging from the mist, the ghost of a dead mother and the baby stood in front of her. The ghost was too scary to watch, and for a beautiful girl like her, it was worse than a nightmare! She screamed and ran into the woods where she found herself accompanied by the unseen residents: the owls!

She heard to the hooting owls those resided on the branches of the enormous trees. Gazing at the trees those swayed along with the freezing winds, she could hardly convince herself that she wasn't afraid.

Loretta was moving further.

The mist revealed the entrance of a massive fort, intriguing her to discover its secrets, and when she passed through it, the cool breezes of the wind were welcoming her in profound quietness.

Entering into the fort, Loretta stood gazing at the ancient artwork on the walls. She moved her eyes to the time-worn interior and the burning candles.

Suddenly, a whitish semi-transparent figure of a lady appeared in front of her. She was a ghost with candles in her hand, who moved into the next chamber. Loretta trailed her and stood in the darkness; she couldn't see the lady but heard her calling her name repeatedly.

'Loretta . . . Loretta . . . Loretta,' whispered the ghost.

CHAPTER 2

Loretta Costigan awoke slowly.

After seeing a terrible nightmare, the whispers of a ghost persisted in her ears. A white cloth tied around her eyes was evidencing her blindness. Her hair was long and somewhat curly. She felt the warmness of the sunlight that entered the window and playfully splattered encompassing her in tender and bliss. Loretta was seventeen-year-old; blind since she was born. She was a wealthy girl leaving in a two-story house.

Her servant called Bessie was a thirty-five-year-old woman, who entered the bedroom with morning refreshments. She was quite concerned about her health. 'Are you feeling well, Miss Loretta?' she asked.

'Yes, I am fine. The medication relieved me from a headache last night.'

Since Loretta was blind, Bessie had her commanding presence. She came closer and tied

Loretta's hair in a bow. Then, she held her palm in her's. 'You should walk this way please.'

Bessie helped her walk to the bath. As soon as Loretta went in the bathtub, Bessie sat near her to help her sponge with the soap. The bath comprised of several scents and Rose petals.

The Roses - one of the greatest fantasies she ever has had. She loved the fragrance of Roses ardently; she could feel the smoothness of the petals, but had no idea how they looked? Her sheer fantasies were not only limited to the flowers but also, she wondered how the froth looked?

Just now, she joyfully experienced the titillation of a soft lather over her naked skin, which drifted gently down her spine and finally into the water. The refreshing redolence of the oil that Bessie poured on her shoulders has reinvigorated her senses, and later, the images of the massacred people plagued her with worriment.

Loretta gasped a heavy breath. She couldn't efface the images those were flashing in her remembrance. Those images were haunting her mind so badly that she wished she could sleep again.

But then, the probability of seeing a nightmare alarmed her with terror.

The streaming blood and the heads of humans she had seen in the dream were unnerving. Since she was blind, she only knew the names of colours but had no idea how each of them looked.

'Bessie, what's the difference between water and blood?'

Bessie stopped sponging for a while. What would she tell her? The water has no colour, and blood

7

looks red? And definitely, the next question would be how "red" looked?

'Basically, water has no colour,' Bessie replied. 'But blood has a colour called Red. Humans and animals carry blood in their bodies.'

Now, there was a relatively gentle smile on Loretta's face. 'I have hopefully found the colour of blood. I have seen it in the nightmare.'

'You saw a bad dream?' Bessie wondered.

'Yes, the soldiers were hunting humans. Kids were crying uncontrollably, and a woman was shot dead. It was truly horrible.'

'Don't worry; it was just a disturbing dream.'

'No, it wasn't just a dream. It carries a message, and I guess there will be a war in the future.'

'Loretta, I suggest not to think about it.'

'Sorry Bessie, but I can't be a negligent citizen, especially when the town is under threat. I need to inform the minister about this.'

Loretta's decision to tell the minister about the nightmare seemed to be like a juvenile. Last night, Loretta didn't go to bed on time, and Bessie thought that the sleep deprivation was the real reason for the nightmare. She didn't believe in dreams. When Loretta was emphasising the fact, Bessie suggested her to talk with her parents. It seemed as if she refrained from her involvement in this matter.

After a rejuvenating bath, Bessie helped her wear a beautiful linen and covered her eyes with a cloth. Her lover always told her how attractive she looked, but unfortunately, she wasn't able to see her beauty in the mirror.

Bessie moisturised her linen with a refreshing scent.

'This is a classy fragrance,' Loretta said.

'It's a Rose perfume.'

'It's Leonardo's favourite.'

Bessie smiled at her and palmed her shoulders. 'So, Mrs. Leonardo, I will be back in a moment.'

Loretta felt shy and grinned cheerfully.

The feelings have been interlacing Loretta's life deeply. Among her five senses, one was eliminated, and the rest contributed well to take the pleasures of life. Slowly, her mind immersed in the memories of her lover, who had tenderly kissed her for the first time.

She remembered the heart-touching feelings when she had spent a romantic wintry night with Leonardo. With long gasps and sensual whispers, she had invited him to discover the secrets of lust and revel in the heavenly pleasures of her sensuality. She wished the night would never end.

Loretta's lips curved into a charming smile after remembering the romantic moments, and suddenly she withdrew herself from the memories after hearing to Bessie's voice.

'Loretta,' Bessie said, 'your mother has prepared your favourite breakfast.' She grasped her palm and descended the stairs to the dining room where Mr. and Mrs. Costigan was waiting for her. *Morning!*

Loretta was envisaging the drama that her mother might create after asking for the permission to meet the minister. She believed that she would counteract her statement strongly. However, she gave it a try by describing the nightmare to her.

Her mother, Edyth, said one thing after listening to the bad dream. 'There is nothing to fear. Forget it.'

Loretta wasn't satisfied by the answer. She was forcing her mother to believe in the dreams, at least the one that she saw. 'My dreams are the indications of the forthcoming. They carry a message, and you know that very well.' Loretta said.

Loretta's father, Jean, was listening to her. He would not at any time tolerate such a nuisance, and he never did. 'I am sorry, but I am not in conformity with your inconsequential predictions,' her father interfered.

Who believe in dreams? Dreams weren't supposed to be true. Dreams were the memories or the illusions. They were the hallucinations, a kaleidoscope of events in the unconscious state of mind. They couldn't be specified or contemplated for why they struck one's mind.

However, in the case of Loretta, something was unique and undefined.

During the time she was born, nature had designed her aura, brain, mind, and her body in such a way that she could perceive the occurrences of the forthcoming events or the past in her dream. According to Loretta, the town was in danger, but her words left no impact on her parents, and their opinion regarding her was entirely negative.

'Loretta,' Edyth said, 'are you out of your mind?'

Edyth was an indifferent woman. Ordinary people in this world have been pointing out the mistakes of the clever. They always told them that the glass was half empty, but never tried to discover the remaining part that was filled with wonders.

'I am not out of my mind,' Loretta raised her voice. 'When I was thirteen, I predicted my brother's death, and he died.' She tried to make them aware of the incident that had taken away the peace from her family. She wept with crushing disappointment. She was expecting her parents to believe in her dream, but they were reacting as if they weren't so serious about it. They preferred to emphasise the truth rather than believing in a dream.

'Loretta, I am sorry. That was merely a coincidence. If we were in danger, the minister would be the first person to know every information regarding the attack. And he knows how to deal with the enemies and avert confrontation,' her mother convinced.

'War isn't the only fear. I have seen a mother dying helplessly. At present, Mrs. Lanchester is pregnant, which means something strange may happen after giving birth to a baby,' Loretta said.

'Enough,' Jean yelled and stood up. 'Nobody is going to talk about nightmares anymore. Do you want people to make fun of you? I expect you to live within the reality, and not in the dreams.'

'Jean,' Edyth said with a concerned gesture. 'I will handle this.'

Jean Costigan left.

Edyth sat beside Loretta and palmed her shoulders. 'Don't worry. I will talk to the minister. I am now going to the church. See you in the afternoon.'

Edyth left the house.

Loretta was sanguine enough that her mother would hardly comply with the needful action. She commanded Bessie to take her to the minister's palace.

The wintry winds were changing as the beams of sunlight descending through the mesh of the trees started to warm up the environment. The chariot moved on the winding paths between the woods and through the morning mist. Loretta was doing what her mind was telling her to do. When Loretta and Bessie reached the minister's palace, a beautiful servant escorted them to the guest room where they waited for Alfred Lanchester, the minister.

This morning, Alfred Lanchester had visited the cathedral that resembled an ancient monument famous for its incredible and unique structure. The religious people believed that their prayers came into existence after the refinement of the soul. And thus, they have gathered in the house of God to hearken to the religious theories.

Next to the idol of Christ, a philosopher has conducted the religious lecture. Alfred closed his eyes, petitioning for the betterment of his life. He was hearkening to the theory of the philosopher.

'God resides in every part of the universe. People praise the idols but forget that God indeed dwells in humans. They betray their beloved ones and expect God to forgive them. Why should God always be glorified for forgiveness? He has given us the powerful tool called as *the brain* that can understand the difference between the merits and sins in consideration with their consequences. What is God? God is joy in itself, and we must find Him within ourselves. He is the creator of the universe, and hence, none of His creations is useless. Every creation has to tell you something. The mountains, rivers, valleys, and everything around you symbolise something. One must have a heart as great as the mountain. The love between people must flow towards each other in abundance like a river. And the thoughts must have the deepness as the valley,' the philosopher said.

A few people applauded while others took a nap. In Alfred's opinion, the speech was a somnolent religious composition. As he got involved in his thoughts, his ears began to miss the words. And then, a whisper woke him suddenly.

'Sir, a young lady wants to meet you. She is waiting inside the palace,' a messenger whispered.

'Tell her to visit tomorrow.'

'I told her, but she is carrying an important message. She wants to deliver it to you in privacy and immediately,' the messenger said.

This kind of message delivery was a custom before the war with a purpose to secure veiled information relating to the antagonists. Moving out of the church, Alfred Lanchester sat in his chariot, and the charioteer sped up the horses.

Entering into the palace, Alfred got introduced to Loretta Costigan and Bessie.

'Mr. Lanchester,' Loretta spoke confidently, 'my nightmare has taken peace and tranquillity far from me, and I am afraid it will take the same away from you. I dreamt of enemies attacking our town. Please don't mind Mr. Lanchester, but I believe I have an auxiliary sense that helps me prognosticate the future.

'What do you mean?'

'My dreams become true. I fear to the enemy's attack and annihilation of the town. Moreover, your wife is pregnant, and I have seen a mother dying helplessly, which means something strange may happen after she gives birth to a baby.'

'You say you saw the future in your dream?'

'Yes, sir.'

'Have you seen my wife?'

'I am not sure.'

'Well, you should not worry about it. I have an ultimate way of fortification that will never let the town enter the gloom of misery,' Alfred said. As a minister, he was judging the circumstances on practical evidence. He had become a minister with the implementation of his winning strategies, which made him overconfident about the possessions those could certainly hold him in trouble. And considering his social eminence and dignity, Loretta didn't emphasise this fact.

'Alright Mr. Lanchester, I hope you will do the needful,' Loretta said. She left along with Bessie.

Alfred didn't believe in the dreams. However, he was a man of many dreams. He wanted his supporters to grow with prosperity. Alfred never showed disbelief in religion and God, but there were a few leaders who withdrew themselves from the existing religion and joined the sorcerers.

Alfred considered the nightmare as the warning since he was aware of his ancestor's real-life story. He started to remember the events those have happened in the past.

CHAPTER 3

Thirty years before –

The evil art of sorcery was originated in Mexico and widespread in many countries. Sorcerers explored different countries and cities extensively and provoked the people to worship evil. Alfred's father, Seymour Lanchester, was one of the pupils who learnt black magic and started performing magic shows on the streets for daily wages.

One day during the performance, Seymour Lanchester spelt an antique mirror with his incredible art of magic and turned it into an unbreakable article. He asked people around to come forward and break the mirror by any means. Most of the people threw stones at it, but nothing could shatter the mirror.

A year later, when Seymour turned forty-year-old, he flipped the pages of the book that his teacher had gifted him. He remembered the words of his master vaguely. *'After the death of a human, the spirit travels far away into the infinity. This book contains spells those the spirits can hear, and they can decide if they want to come back to the real world to complete their wishes. Many sorcerers use these spells during the ghost calling ritual.'*

Sitting in the spectacular glints of candle-lights, he tried to call the wandering spirits without the expert's supervision. Soon, the bewilderedness shook him with terror when the blood-drops fell on the pages. He sat bolt upright and gazed at the ceiling with a deep gasp; frightened and terrorised. The weird appearance of scary mother and her baby have left him shivering. They were stuck on the roof like the lizards. They were unblinkingly staring at him with rage and fierce. Their white eyes looked scary, and their grey bodies leaked the drops of blood from the wounds. He began to read the next spell to send them to their origin, but the book went on fire immediately. The ghost disappeared after the combustion of the book, and Seymour resolutely decided not to play with the spells again.

*   *   *

Fear being the worst emotion of the universe was not only limited to humans but also, it grasped the animals. Even the spirits feared! The fear had its faces.

Fear of losing beloved.

Fear of punishment.

Fear of dark and death.

However, it was immensely powerful feeling that could transform life from pleasure to hell, from happiness to wretchedness.

Tonight, the ghost of the mother haunted Morgane's Park and sat on the lawn with the baby to her chest. Her face was hiding in the dark despite the moonlight. She was singing a song as bloodcurdling as the death, or even worse than anyone could imagine.

Her baby wanted to sleep desperately; it was dead for a long time, but it wasn't sleeping. Her gown was dusty, and her hair was long. She looked scary, and she was now crying, counting the days she had lived after the death.

She remembered how she died. She couldn't forget her brutal murderers. Their sin-stained souls were smelling.

She could smell them now and then.

She got up and walked on the lawn, her gown waving over the grass, leaving behind the trails of blood.

She sat in the darkness of graveyard, groaning and digging her grave where her body was left to decompose after her death. She was cursed, she couldn't use her body to live again, yet she was leaving life, free from death.

Now, she was sitting before her body, burning in the wrenching pain, until the outburst of revenge aroused and turned her insane.

*   *   *

Christelle was the wife of Seymour; beautiful, loving, and caring. She was alone in the house. An hour after the dawn, the darkness swallowed the streets but not her house as many glistening candles have brightened the room. Standing near the closed window and gazing out at the streets, she was figuring out which among the passing chariots belonged to her husband.

A few miles away, the ball dancers have haunted the party where Christelle was invited, and after waiting for Seymour for too long, her perseverance came to an end. He never took so long to get back from work. Christelle had dressed in a long corset Edwardian gown for the party. She had no idea where her husband was dawdling instead of hurrying to home.

After a few moments, she stepped away from the window, and then, the windows opened, giving way to the wintry wind that blew away all the candles, and in a fraction of seconds, the darkness grappled the house. Christelle lighted a candle and stood in the centre of the room; terrified and frightened to see two shadows on the wall; one was of her own, and the other belonged to the unseen entity that had entered the house.

The ghost blew away the candle by creating a blowing sound, and then, a sudden upheaval of fear made her scream like an insane. A moment later, she felt someone grabbing her feet. She tried to run but fell on the floor. Finally, the unseen entity gripped her legs tightly and dragged her into the bedroom. Christelle couldn't do anything except screaming for help.

About an hour later, Seymour broke into the house and called her name with ambiguity as the darkness upsurged the suspicion of her safety.

'Christelle, where are you?' he bellowed and tried to find her in the candle-light.

'I am here!' She said.

He moved anxiously towards the dark bedroom as her voice had an unusual excitement and turned thicker than before. Stepping ahead stealthily, he scanned the bedrooms scrupulously in the candlelight and found her hanging to the roof upside down with the long trails of uncomely hair.

Slipping on the matted floor with wide opened eyes, Seymour sensed a cramp in his heart as the ghost burst out with unremitting laughter. She jumped on the ground and propelled untamed to break his skull. Soon, he pushed her on the bed and fastened her hands and legs with the ropes.

Seymour somehow succeeded to have temporary control over her, but he has to find help forthwith. He rushed to his chariot in a flash and rode the horses at great velocity. In a few minutes, he brought a priest and told everything about the witchcraft unhesitatingly.

'You should not have tried the spells without the supervision of an expert,' the priest said.

'I am sorry. Please find some way to get rid of this ghost,' Seymour requested.

'I can free your wife from the clutches of the evil, but that will be a temporary solution,' the priest said.

Seymour had read books on exorcism and capturing the ghost, and he believed that the spirit, if not freed from the world, can be caught by something. And then, the thought of the mirror struck his mind instantaneously.

'Can we trap the ghost in the unbreakable mirror?' he asked.

'Yes. That is the only way to keep you and your wife away from the ghost,' the priest said.

Seymour uncovered the mirror and placed it in front of the bed where his wife was mourning continuously. The priest began the exorcism by sprinkling holy water on her body. During the process, her deafening screams ruined the peace of night. Her nerves and body swelled and contracted grotesquely at time intervals. When she stared at the mirror, the fumes emerging from the mouth went into it and brought her in the normal state. Seymour covered the mirror, placed in the chariot, and rode along the bridle path that took him to the Gaston Fort – the fort that Loretta Costigan had discovered in the nightmare. The fort was an abandoned monument, yet he entered inside and hung the mirror on the wall and left.

* * *

After a few days, the time had come when Seymour had to owe Norman, his teacher, the price for lending him the knowledge of sorcery. Norman visited his residence with the same purpose.

'Tell me, master, what do you want?' asked Seymour.

'I wish to marry your sister,' Norman demanded.

Seymour felt like standing in the earthquake. 'This is impossible. She is only twenty-three-year-old, and she is already in love with a man of her age.'

'I know, but this is what you must owe me. Take your time and think again,' said the teacher and walked away.

The demand of the teacher was not convincing him to pay such a price to learn the evil art. After all, the unfeeling teacher had no veneration towards humanity. Since the beginning, Seymour had kept his wife in the dark, and his numerous prevarications lead him to pay the debt. Once, his teacher had asked him to contaminate his soul by his liaison with a strumpet called Lavender. Today, Seymour remembered what he had done in the past.

*   *   *

Lavender was beautiful, the darling of all royal leaders and the kings. Her Victorian corset-ball-gown was glamorous. Her hair was blonde and curly. Her benevolence for the poor was conspicuously unusual, and today it was being observed by the royal dictators. She walked on the streets, feeding the poor; children, adults, and senior citizens, who were overwhelmed by her generosity, and they said, 'Look, she is the angel. The one and only who cares for the impoverished.'

Standing in the crowd, Seymour saw her bestowing gifts to the children. Their faces blossomed with smiles, and no matter what she was doing for her earnings, she was, however, gratifying the souls of the beggars. They were the children of God! They should be cared and loved. As she walked further, their guardians with tears of joy blessed her from the bottom of their hearts.

That night when the moon shone with lustre, and the stars in the dark infinity dazzled with splendour; Seymour Lanchester waited outside the king's castle with a resolute determination to meet the wise lady. He now perceived a figure that was emerging from the mist. She was arriving on a white horse with a flaming torch in her hand. She halted and stepped down from the horse and walked further ignoring him.

'*Lavender, you are a wise woman,*' Seymour said, drawing her attention to him.

She stopped. '*How do you know my name?*'

'*I can hardly find anybody in this town who don't know about you.*'

'*What do you want?*'

'*You are here for the king. After having born in the sophisticated family, what made you a strumpet?*'

'*The wealth that my family earns restricts me to make endowments to the poor. To my knowledge, what I am doing is not a sin. My morals tell me that I must satisfy the needs of impoverished, no matter if the dictators propose me to sacrifice my maidenhood to them, I, however, remain a genuine person. In fact, the dictators are obliged to take care of the people, but they hardly follow the principles of the throne. They are misusing their wealth by spending it on salacious whores. If I endear myself to them instead, all the money that I earn can be used for the nourishment of the poor.*'

'*You are not only wise but a great woman I have ever met in my life.*'

'*I am pleased to hear that. So, what made you come here?*'

'*I was thinking to hire you, but your generosity and sacrifice are priceless.*'

'*You can pay me anything that comes in your possession.*'

Seymour produced a moneybag and spoke, '*This is for the needy.*'

Miles away in the old farmhouse, they were regaling themselves with grapes and kisses. The fireplace provided them with the light as they took pleasures in the raw. Sensually high, the procreating sounds reverberated the *rooms as they traversed lustful fantasies with voluptuous pleasure, and at the peak of their intimacy, they gasped a long breath with utmost gratification.*

*   *   *

The dawn had just about broken with the happy chirp of birds. Seymour's sister, Millicent, was taken back to Blitzland after the tour. She was sitting near the window of the chariot; her eyes shone with cheerfulness while taking the pleasure of serene nature. Moving on the mountain paths, she gazed at the dusty haze at the horizon. The rising sun seemed diminished at first, and gradually, it transformed into a glowing sphere.

An hour later, Millicent reached her home and embraced her dear brother. At that moment, Seymour was hiding his embarrassment with an artificial smile.

'You should marry Augustine at the earliest,' Seymour said.

'I am glad to hear that,' she said, expressing the joy with a great smile on her face like the blossomed lotus in the glint of the wintry sun. She was unaware of the fact that Seymour was liable to pay the price of his wrongdoing, and if Norman succeeds to execute his relentless decision, she has to suffer wrenching life for no reason. Though her marriage with Augustine was the way out, it was not a one day task.

'I would like to meet him. Can you take me to him?' Seymour demanded.

'Of course, I can. But, what is the matter?' she asked. Till now, Seymour showed no interest in their marriage, and all of a sudden he changed his mind.

'I am sorry, I can't tell you. I want to meet him now.'

'No. It is not fair to hide anything from me, after all, I am your little sister. Am I not?'

'Of course, you are, and I love you so much.'

'Then why are you hesitating?'

'I will tell you everything in the right place at the right time. Trust me and take me to Augustine,' he said.

On his forceful plea, Millicent trod along with him to the chariot, sat beside him, and the charioteer moved the chariot towards Augustine's house. Riding on somewhat bouncy bridle path through the foggy timberlands and the over the bridges, they reached Augustine's house that was beige and surrounded by greenery.

When Augustine opened the door after hearing the knocks on it, he was quite surprised by their appearance. He didn't expect them to visit his house early this morning. Millicent stepped ahead and embraced him tightly.

'Don't worry, he wants us to get married at the earliest,' she said. Her lips curved into a smile.

For Augustine, it was like a dream coming true. 'Are you serious?'

'Yes. Ask him if I am kidding,' she said.

Augustine looked deep into his eyes. 'I hope this is not your deliberate lie. What made you change your mind?'

Seymour gasped a breath with embarrassment. He thought Augustine would celebrate after hearing the good news, but he was interrogating him instead.

Augustine knew very well that the one who learns sorcery has to pay a heavy toll to the master after pursuing the knowledge, and most of the sorcerers would try to enchant young women from the families of their pupil.

The first news was good, followed by the worst. Seymour explained, 'Time has changed. I want both of you to get married right now in the church and leave Blitzland forever.'

Millicent interfered, 'Wait a moment. Why are you telling us to move out of the town?'

Augustine was staring at him doubtfully.

'The sorcerer who taught me the art of black magic wants to marry you,' Seymour told her.

Millicent stood in shock and couldn't believe that this was her brother talking to her. Now, the tears filled her eyes and the mind with disquietness. She spoke with revulsion, 'You are a disgrace to me. You made a deal with him without considering my pride as if I did not suppose to be a self-esteemed woman but a mannequin of your indecent show.'

'Millicent, I was unaware of his uncompassionate frame of mind and his outlook towards my family.'

Augustine felt strange about this fact. He interfered, 'Mr. Lanchester, your imprudence has made both of us to face the peril of evil art. Did you ever know that your teacher can bewitch your sister by using a voodoo doll?'

'How do you know about sorcery in detail?' Seymour asked.

'I used to be a sorcerer in my teenage,' Augustine replied.

'Then, you must be knowing the way to get rid of this,' Seymour said.

'Burn you teacher alive,' Augustine replied.

*   *   *

The night was dark and frightening. The house was burning in flames. People stood gazing at it, and they said, 'The Ghost has punished him. You are likely to invite your death when you play with the spells.'

Long at a distance, Seymour caught spy on the teacher's wife as she ran lamentingly toward her house. To save the teacher, a few courageous and kind men entered into the flames with their bodies covered in blankets. They brought the teacher out of the house and laid him on the ground. The teacher was counting the last moments of his life. He gave his wife a golden key and told her about its secret.

After a few days, Seymour broke into her new house, and with a knife, he threatened her to leak out the information on the secret of the key.

'I don't know anything. Only what he asked me was to secure the key,' she said.

'Now, this will remain in my possession,' he said, grabbing the key.

After a few months, she gave birth to a baby and named him Carlton. When Carlton turned eighteen-year-old, she told him the secret of the key.

At the other hand, Seymour's son, Alfred, was twelve-year-old. Seymour said that the key was precious, not because it was made out of gold, but it was meant to protect his generation.

CHAPTER 4

No matter how much you adore a cub with sympathy, when it grows into a lion, it shows its true nature. Today, Alfred Lanchester knew that the jaws of the evils were hungry to swallow the wise. He had no plans regarding Carlton Stoker as of now, but Loretta's nightmare had left him with discomfort. His subordinate, Rex Vabsley, was an authoritative leader, who came to meet him with a purpose of Blitzland's fortification.

'Mr. Lanchester, I have an exclusive news, but it is not a good one,' Rex Vabsley said.

Alfred Lanchester knew very well that Carlton Stoker practised evil rituals, after all, he was the son of a sorcerer.

'Do you want to notify me about Carlton's strategy?' he asked.

'Exactly. Carlton is an ingenious Democrat, and his continuous efforts to bring your death will benefit other dictators. However, they are in conformity with each other in regards to their unique strategies and plans,' Rex Vabsley said.

'Dictators! They all share similar temperaments. They can do anything for their political benefit and self-worth. However, they cannot ruin their widespread reputation by committing crimes, especially when they are dwelling in democracy,' Alfred said.

'I agree with your remark, Mr. Lanchester, but the dictators are no threat to you. The real monster is Carlton Stoker,' Rex said.

'Carlton won't kill me, not until I tell him where the key is,' Alfred said. Rex looked at him inquisitively as his curiosity grew to acknowledge the information on the golden key, but Alfred didn't speak further on that subject. 'By the way, is there anything else you want to share with me?

'I have got something to tell you, Mr. Lanchester. Carlton is not only your enemy but also an inveterate subverter of the religious laws. He is provoking the townies to commit crimes by the means of sorcery. When I was coming here, I witnessed a man burning in the flames. I rushed to save his life, but he was already dead.'

Alfred gazed at him with absolute consternation as he got a hint that Carlton would do every possible thing that comes in his power to acquire blessings from the evil. Moreover, people in that era were turning into unscrupulous humans or predators by sacrificing men and women to the evil and eating their flesh as a part of respect towards the ritual. Greedy people were never happy with whatever they possessed, and a few intended to take revenge by shedding blood of their beloved family members due to the rising personal conflicts and threats. Alfred desired to visit the place where the man was burnt alive. Grabbing a rifle, he trailed Rex Vabsley on a horse.

They reached in the heart of woods and halted in the fearful silence. Alfred's eyes grew in terror as he stared at the body that seemed like a log of charcoal on the dusty ground.

'This is horrible,' Alfred said.

'Let's find if there are more bodies excluding this one,' Rex said.

Riding further, they came across the fencing of the graveyard and halted again. The bridle path lay across the graves, taking further to the abandoned castle. The graveyard was too scary to venture, filled with dark rocks and bare trees.

'Have you ever been to the castle?' Rex asked.

'No. When I was a teenager, I always wondered about its spooky appearance. I was always curious to know what lay inside, but never crossed the graves,' Alfred said.

'Now it's time to venture farther,' Rex said, stepping down from the horse and opening the gate.

Their apprehension fluttered through them as they went ahead, bringing vividly to their mind the growing deeper silence. The soil was dark here, filled with fossils of humans and animals, and they kept moving further till they reached the castle.

Partly shaded and somewhat lighted with fire torches, the walls held ancient paintings those beautifully illustrated the people kneeling before naked goddess and other incredible artworks.

'This is a magnificent piece of art,' Alfred said, staring at the naked goddess.

'I like all of them. These paintings belonged to the artists from the medieval era,' Rex said.

'Have you ever been here?'

'Not really. The style of the art is showing how old they are.'

'You have a great knowledge of art.'

'I am pleased to hear that.'

Soon, they heard the voice of a moaning woman, who was hanging on the ceiling in a net. She was a virtuous woman dressed in the Edwardian gown. When she was riding through the forest, she told them, Carlton and his guards seized her to offer her flesh to the evil.

After listening to her plea, all they could do to save her life was to shoot the rope and grab her in their arms.

*　　*　　*

The blazing candles splattered magnificent golden glints in the bedroom where Alfred's wife, Florence, who was nine-month-old pregnant, lay sprawled on the bed. She had two assistants, Madeleine, and Martina, who helped her in all the household work from breakfast to bed. They were beautiful sisters. Madeleine was an eighteen-year-old girl; responsible and matured, and Martina was leaving in the fantasies of fifteen.

Florence was habituated to read books before sleeping, and the one she was reading tonight, was kind of interesting.

'Mrs. Lanchester, the book you are reading is a romance novel with a word of advice to lovers, and we are eagerly waiting for you to feed our imagination,' Madeleine said.

'Imagination! Can you imagine life without a partner?' Florence asked.

'To be honest, no.' Madeleine said.

'This is a story about a lady who lived a long wrenching life after losing her husband. She struggled for her daily wages. A few wealthy people assumed that she was interested in remarrying the one who offered her a proposal. She could have lived a prosperous life if she hadn't rejected him,' Florence said.

'Why she didn't marry him?' Martina asked.

Madeleine looked at Martina and spoke, 'She kept her promise.'

Florence glanced at her and said, 'You are right. For her, marriage was not only a conjugation of physical bodies for pleasures but also a devotion of souls. When she got married in the church, she considered God as the witness and gave her husband her mind, body, and soul. His death was some loyalty test for her, and standing before God, she wished to marry him again in the next life.'

'Great story, though, filled with emotions and morals. I believe, your child will grow into a famous lover,' Martina said.

Florence softly refused, 'I don't want my baby to become one among the famous lovers as most them lost their beloved ones or sacrificed their lives for their partners.'

'So, every famous love story is a tragedy,' Madeleine said.

'Not necessary. By the way, what about your love story? Have you replied to Wilfred's proposal?'

'Not yet.'

'Do you like him?' Florence asked.

The shyness on Madeleine's face was quite feminine. Her eyes went down as she stood in silence for a moment, and then, she answered, 'Yes. I like him. He is out of the town, and I will meet him when he comes back,' Madeleine said.

'Make sure you fix a date,' Florence said.

Madeleine nodded and said, 'Shall we leave?'

Florence nodded.

When Madeleine and Martina stepped out, they smiled at Alfred, who was heading towards the bedroom, carrying the rifle on his shoulder. Alfred stepped into the bedroom closing the door behind him.

'Did you go to the forest?' Florence questioned, gazing at the rifle that he was hanging on the wall.

'Yes. There was a death investigation. A man was burnt alive.'

'God! Who was the culprit?'

'Carlton Stoker is the suspect, but we have found no shreds of evidence till now.'

'What are you going to do now?'

'Wait for the opportunities. However, I have ordered Rex Vabsley to collect more information on the sorcerers.'

Florence sighed in weariness. For her, life was a melodrama, full of perturbations and mysteries.

* * *

The night had gotten dark enough; the mist was covering the earth's crust as far as the eyes could reach. The hooting owls hiding in the branches seemed to forewarn the possibilities of danger. This moment was suspicious, risky, and could turn worse than anyone had imagined. About an hour before, Rex Vabsley had received Alfred's order, and he doubted that the sorcerers carried evil rituals at the abandoned castle. He wanted to find the truth. He was now patrolling the forest on a horse with a rifle. To his knowledge, the art of sorcery was performed with human sacrifice. Some said that the sorcerers burnt people alive during the rituals. A few rumours have ruffled among the townies that witchcraft involved bare dancers, who performed a wicked dance before the fire in absorbing the heat. Then, that heat would become the power and could be transformed to the sorcerers after their liaison with them. Though they were rumours, every wise person spoke about destroying the witches.

As Rex moved further into the dark woods, he witnessed three chariots making their way through a bridle path, and by trailing them without drawing their attention, he passed the graveyard and stood at a distance from the castle. Now, those three chariots belonged to Carlton Stoker, who appeared to be a cruel person.

Stepping out from the chariot like a warrior, Carlton raised his voice on the guards. 'Don't wait for my orders. You know what to do.'

The guards nodded. They pulled out an old man from the cabin and whipped him with a stick.

'Stop it, please. What have I done to you?' the old man cried.

'You denied our request. We have asked your daughter to help us in the ritual. And you helped her escaping the town,' a guard said.

'We are going to cook you on fire,' said another guard, without knowing that he was Rex Vabsley's target. And in the next moment, the bullet tore his ribs and killed him.

A moment after the gunfire, the guards hastened to hide. This attack was unexpected, and the old man was taking more of its advantage as he escaped in a chariot. Then, there was numerous encounters and bloodshed. Rex Vabsley killed almost all the guards. He intended to shoot Carlton Stoker, but his rifle went empty. Carlton was fortunate enough to survive. Since the beginning of the attack till the end, none of the bullets went through him.

The fight had ended.

It was dark enough, and Rex thought that there was no point in staying there alone. In no time intervening, he rode his horse and reached his home. Gasping harder, he stepped into his house closing the door behind him, and standing for a moment of silence; he gazed at his beautiful wife, Jeanette, who was writing a letter in the candle-lights. Her Edwardian gown was a magnificent art of fashion, one of the favourites of Rex.

She glanced at him and said, 'You look tired.'

Rex was looking at her in wonderment. After surviving a devastating chaos, she could only see him tired.

'You have no idea what I have been through,' he spoke calmly.

'What happened?'

'I confronted the black magician.'

'You mean Carlton Stoker?'

'You know much about him.'

'He is the only threat to the town, and all that I know about him is because of you. You should not be too ambitious to risk your life,' Jeanette said.

For Rex, life didn't seem worthy without risk. He would have made brilliant plans of the annihilation of the culprits, and those would have minimised the risk. 'I was following the commands of the minister. Do you think I am wrong at any point?'

'Not really. But it doesn't mean that you should risk your life.'

'I was prepared for every contingency. After all, I am a warrior with courage and kindness. You know very well; someone has to take the initiative to step into the battle of justice to salvage the humankind.'

'I never stopped you from fighting against injustice. Only what I am trying to say is, you take too much of risk than others do,' Jeanette explained.

'Alright. I will implement your suggestions. Happy now?' Rex said, leaning forward to kiss her from behind.

Jeanette smiled, turning around to meet his lips.

No doubt, Rex Vabsley was a kind person. But his kindness, loyalty, and determination towards duty were on the pernicious edge tonight. This night was full of terror that left no signs to predetermine of what would come next. His mind had dived into the depth of slumber, without giving him a hint that his wife had stepped out of the house, and ventured into the jaws of the death. She had sensed someone wandering outside the house, and by holding an oil lamp, she was too anxious to discover the hidden faces in the dark. Her eyes stretched wide with terror after facing armed men.

She stepped back and leant on a massive chest of the most brutal sorcerer – Carlton Stoker. He masked her face and abducted her in a chariot.

Tonight, the clouds overshadowed the moon. The owls were hooting louder. The drizzle transformed into an intense thunderstorm, and the lightening was living, dying, and reliving with extreme flashiness. It seemed as if the Gods were shedding tears from the heaven, expressing their tremendous grief for the one they loved. Tonight, the jaws of death were swallowing the wise, and there was nobody to listen to her plea. There was nobody to help her, though, she was struggling to make an escape. She realised that her efforts were lacking the strength of her fortune, or maybe the sins from the past were leading her to a grievous misfortune.

Jeanette was a true believer of God. Tonight, it was proven that even Gods couldn't emancipate his devotees from the fate of death, nor do they come in the visible form, but they have always made the world feel their presence.

Rex Vabsley awoke after hearing to one of the thunders, and soon, realised that Jeanette was missing. The door that was left open was the indication that she had ventured out in the dark, and all he could do was to go in quest of her on the horse.

It was raining heavily.

Rex Vabsley had no idea what had happened to her? Where had she gone? Every moment felt like a breathtaking adventure in the dark. Till now, only a few people talked about wild animals living in the forest, and Rex had been taking it as their assumption. It only required a few howling wolfs for him to believe the fact that wildlife existed there. Rex stopped the horse and drew the rifle expeditiously. The wolfs were not seen in the dark, but their howls defined how close they were getting. In the flash of the lightening, the face of a wolf became visible, and in the fraction of a moment, Rex shot the animal dead. Then the second one came closer and jumped in the air but couldn't make it to him. After the third takedown, everything went silent. Rex gasped a breath and rode his horse further.

Rex doubted on the sorcerers he had previously met, and the thought of human sacrifice was bringing to him a despair of her being alive. The fear that clutched his heart was overpowering as he reached the abandoned castle.

Rex stood at the doorstep and partly opened the door and gazed inside at the naked women those have surrounded the burning woods. They were dancing and singing songs for the evil. For the first time, Rex was witnessing a creepy ritual of the witches. Perhaps, the townies knew about their existence and the way they enjoyed the bloodbath. Rex gripped his rifle tightly and shot all of them one after the other. When everyone died, the woods extinguished without any physical means, and the darkness swallowed the entire castle.

Rex pushed the large door to its creaky noise and advanced in the darkness toward one of the chambers. Suddenly, a dead body came down from the ceiling and fell hard on the floor. He gazed at the corpses those were hanging to the roof. Rex heard someone whispering in the corridors. He moved stealthily. A sudden appearance of a ghost terrified him, and he shot it with the gun. The spirit turned to him and gestured by moving a finger to its mouth.

'Shh,' it said and vanished.

He walked into a dark chamber and witnessed some eyes those sparkled with rage. Rex ran out of the castle as the haunting experiences terrified him. He had set out in search of his wife, which remained incomplete.

Rex Vabsley returned to home empty handed. After enormous efforts, all that he could gather was disappointment and frustration. He gulped glasses after glasses of wine as the night wore on, and finally fell on the floor.

*   *   *

After a stormy night, the sun shone in the sky. Rex opened his eyes as he sensed the sunlight glittering on his face. Every time he awoke, he found Jeanette beside him, but today the bed was empty. Rex got up and gazed at the bronze glass on the floor that held a few drops of wine. He hardly bothered to pick it up. He stood near the window and threw glances at the trees and the herbs those have garmented the surrounding.

It seemed to be a gloomy day in every manner, maybe because the loss of his wife had ruined his peace and tranquillity. Despite his constant endeavour, he barely got any hint of her existence. Moreover, the chances of her survival in the iniquitous world were reducing day after the other. He wondered how could abductors step into the house and get hands on her while she was sleeping next to him? And why didn't they harm him? If there were noise in the room, Rex would have got up from the slumber. So Jeanette must have gone out and fallen pray to her abductors, he guessed.

No matter whatever the case was, the criterion of Jeanette's search and safety had become significant. Rex was looking out of the window, thinking of a better idea to find Jeanette. And in a few minutes, he spotted a chariot stopping in front of his house. Four men stepped out; among them, one was very familiar to him. He was Carlton Stoker.

Then, Rex heard a few knocks on the door. He opened it holding a rifle and precisely aimed Carlton Stoker. 'What are you doing here?' he questioned.

'Come on Mr. Vabsley, as if you don't know anything,' Carlton said.

'Seriously, what are you talking about?' Rex asked.

Carlton smiled. 'You know, sometimes people search for a thing that lies in their pocket.'

Rex moved down the rifle slowly. 'So you know where my wife is.'

'Well, she is in my custody,' Carlton said, stepping into his house. 'You are a wise person, and I doubt you would estrange yourself from your coordinators if you were told to betray anyone among them.'

'What coordinators? What are you talking about?'

'I am speaking about Alfred Lanchester. If you comply with my demands, I will do no harm to your wife.'

Rex began to burn with unrestrained rage. He pointed the rifle at him. 'I can kill you right here right now.'

'Of course, you can, but you won't be able to see your wife anymore.' Carlton was calm since his illegitimate ascendancy over him has turned the circumstances in his favour.

'What you want me to do?'

'Alfred Lanchester has secured a golden key. You have to steal the key and give it to me. I give you my word. Nothing will happen to Jeanette,' Carlton said.

Finally, Rex Vabsley made his mind as there was no option left except betraying the minister.

CHAPTER 5

The dawn had just broken; somewhat silent or filled with the chirps of the birds. Florence stood near the window gazing the spectrum of beautiful nature. The eastern horizon blazed with the hot orange sun, following with the saffron clouds floating in the celestial sphere. Further, the orange colour blended with the new blue sky, diminishing the stars and the moon.

This sunshine brought the most beautiful moments in Florence's life. She knew she would go into confinement for several hours and rise again with the gratification of motherhood.

Today, the rush was inside the minister's palace. A matured lady called Estell, who was a childbirth expert, had come to meditate and help Florence through the confinement.

'I want both of you to assist me,' Estell told Madeleine and Martina. To her command, they locked the door and stood near Florence.

Florence was going through confinement for the first time, and she had no idea how difficult or easy it was to give birth to a child. The growing nervousness on her face was remarkable.

Estell knew what condition she was going through. She told her not to worry about anything. What Florence was lacking was moral support and confidence.

Estell spoke, 'Mrs. Lanchester, don't be scared. During the confinement, most of the women discover their strength and courage to endure the pain, and I am sure, after the birth of the baby, you will feel proud of yourself.'

Florence took a deep breath and spoke, 'Is it not true that the pains are excruciating?'

'Every woman has a different opinion regarding this. If you are talking about the pains, then I must say that you should count it as a gift and not a curse. Now, get rid of your thoughts and take a deep breath,' Estell said.

Florence was following her advice. She was in confinement for several hours. At a point, she broke down into tears.

'Why are you crying? You are doing a good job. The baby is going to see the world because of you,' Estell said.

Florence just nodded.

Estell continued, 'You can talk to me; I am just like your mother. Do you trust me?'

'Yes.' Florence said with tears in her eyes.

Estell's emotional support was strengthening her confidence and courage.

At the final moment, Florence grabbed the bed and screeched as she laboriously pushed the baby through the birth canal, and finally out into the world. Her eyes shined with joy and the great pride of motherhood. Holding the newborn daughter delicately, she smiled with excitement.

'Please call her father,' Florence said.

Through the front window of the palace, Alfred gazed at the morning mist that lay across the dusty streets. Martina greeted him and delivered the message. His mind blossomed with happiness, but the words of Loretta Costigan seemed to overrule his joy: *I have seen a mother dying helplessly, which means something strange may happen after the birth of the baby.*

However, Alfred could hardly wait more than a moment to see Florence and the baby.

That day, another astounding news came to Madeleine through a letter. Her lover, Wilfred, was back in the town, who asked her to meet him the next morning at the lakefront. The happiness that gathered in her heart was remarkably seen on her face.

The next day, when the dawn had just about broken, the charioteer took Madeleine to the lakeshore where Wilfred was waiting. She ran towards him, holding her Edwardian gown above her ankles, and embraced him with a kiss. After a long time, Madeleine was spending a peaceful morning with him by the lakeshore.

She gazed at the orange colour in the eastern sky.

'Wilfred,' she said, 'look at those colours! What a beautiful morning it is! I had been waiting for long to see the sunrise with you. Isn't it romantic?'

'Yes, it is as beautiful as you.'

The chilly breezes were exhilarating her as she walked by the lakeshore. The revitalising smell of the wet sand under her bare feet had done enough to rejoice her senses. The colours of the flowers were enormously beautiful as she merrily jogged towards them. She touched them with her delicate fingers, and then, moved them on the branches and the stems.

She gazed at the tree and listened to the enchanting melodies of the birds. The grass was swinging along with the wind, and the spectrum of nature at its abundance seemed to be smiling at her. Then, she sat with him near the lake. She elevated her gown above her knees and dipped her lovely legs in the water, and swayed them to and fro. She gave a lighthearted laugh when he tickled her hips and navel with his sensual fingers, and with the arousing feelings, she took pleasure of hot smooches in the romantic bed of nature.

When the sun-baked enough, they gave a short farewell to each other. Madeleine sat in the chariot and moved at great velocity. She wondered why the charioteer was in a hurry. Madeleine was sitting inside the wooden cabin that restricted her to talk to him. She thought the charioteer was taking her to the palace, but the truth was bitter than her imagination.

Now, the chariot halted in the woods, and to her surprise, the charioteer was Rex Vabsley, who dragged her out, pushed her to the ground, and threatened her with a flintlock pistol.

'Tell me where the golden key is?' Rex asked.

'I don't know what are you talking about?' Madeleine said fearfully.

'Listen, my wife is in danger, and all I can do to save her is by reaching out to the key.'

'How did you reach out to me?'

'Since last night, Carlton Stoker is spying on me, and I am spying on you. Now, tell me where the key is?'

'It is in the golden box in the palace.'

'And where is that golden box?'

'It is kept in front of the painting of a naked fairy.'

'Where is that naked fairy?'

'Next to the picture of an Egyptian goddess.'

Rex realised that she was misleading him. 'You have a sister, and she is an inviting beauty. Am I right?'

Madeleine didn't want him to persecute Martina at any cost for any reason. She told him that the box was on the last floor of the castle, above the minister's bedroom. Rex sighed in relief. He thought he could save Jonette. But, Madeleine has now become a threat to him, and her death would indeed protect the disclosure of his betrayal to anyone. For a moment, he gasped a heavy breath and shot the bullet into her heart. The blood flowing from her ruptured breast was now flooding through her gown and on the ground. Rex Vabsley carried her body in the chariot and buried it in the misty graveyard.

Madeleine would have never imagined that this was the last sunrise of her life. The last kiss that she had taken from her lover in the bed of peaceful nature. Even nature was sensing her loss as the silence of grief spread along the lakeshore. The birds went silent; the wind has stopped, and the cheerful morning has turned into a misery that remained a secret.

A sudden disappearance of Madeleine has shaken everyone with trepidation and affliction, as a result of which, Alfred commanded his guards to find her, and even after searching every part of the town, they found no sign of her existence. When they returned empty handed, Martina burst into tears.

'Please tell me that she is alive,' she cried.

It was quite hard to believe or assume that she was dead, not at least without seeing her body. Martina was going through a massive torment for the second time. The first one was the death of her parents when she was a child. Since then, her sister was everything to her. She felt like living a cursed life; ruthless and unforgiving in all the ways as she was left completely alone in this selfish world. Martina felt pity for Wilfred. His desire of marrying Madeleine was never going to be true. With every sunrise Wilfred searched the streets and the lakeshore, hoping that he would find her one day.

Though Madeleine was dead, Rex had successfully laid out significant information on the golden key. Right after the darkness fell, he prepared himself for another adventure. Rex was going to steal the key by masking his face and changing the weapon. He didn't want to draw the attention of the townies as the rifle would awake everybody at the wrong time. And to avoid worse circumstances, he chose an appropriate weapon: a crossbow.

Rex carried a bag on his shoulders and walked in the dark.

Tonight, when the entire town rested in slumber, Rex stood at a distance from the palace, hiding behind a tree. He counted the guards at the front door.

'One, two, three.'

He produced three arrows from the bag and shot the first guard.

Now, the death of the first guard unnerved the others. 'Who is there?' a guard said, loading his rifle.

'I am sure there is someone in the woods,' said the other guard.

They proceeded towards the groves, pointing their guns aimlessly in the dark.

Rex didn't want them to shoot or make any noise, which would propagate the rising threat. He had already chosen the other way to make it to the front door.

The guards, when turned around, found him on the doorstep. They pulled the triggers, but Rex somehow saved himself. Finally, he produced a flintlock pistol and shot both of them.

Now, Alfred Lanchester awoke suddenly after the gunfire. He grabbed a rifle and stepped out. Meanwhile, Rex had managed to get into the room where the box was lying. He gazed out of the window at the street and saw Alfred wandering suspiciously.

Alfred Lanchester looked above at the palace and caught his glimpse.

Though Rex ducked immediately, he couldn't escape from his vision. Rex knew that Alfred was hastening towards the room. He dived out of the window with the box and hurt himself. However, he escaped by using the cover of the night.

After reaching home, Rex opened the box and stood with disappointment. It was empty. He flung it on the wall with growing annoyance, regreting Madeleine's death.

The next day, Rex Vabsley walked into the palace and saw Alfred preparing a drink for himself.

'Mr. Lanchester,' Rex said, 'I got your message. It is quite hard to believe someone breaking into the palace last night.'

'Drink?'

'No. Thank you.'

Alfred placed his glass on the table. 'What would be your opinion if I were supposed to make an amendment in the laws?' Alfred turned towards him. 'In my speculation, incarceration of three years in the case of robbery isn't sufficient. The punishment could have been worse to avoid threats.'

'I comply with the requirements, Mr. Lanchester, but it will take some time to get it approved by the jurisdiction.'

'That is why I called you here, Mr. Vabsley. I want to assign you with one more task including Madeleine's case.'

'I am glad that you find me eligible for your most significant operations,' Rex replied.

'Mr. Vabsley, all I want you to do is arrest the thief who intended to steal the key.'

'The key?'

'You know that I have secured it right here in the palace. Fortunately, I have moved it from the box.'

'So you think the thief was trying to get the key?'

Alfred nodded. 'I also believe that Madeleine's abduction has a connection with it. She knew that the key was lying in the box.'

Rex pretended as if he was unaware of Madeleine's disappearance. 'Madeleine's abduction! Are you serious, Mr. Lanchester? She was an excellent caretaker and a friend of your family.'

'I have no idea whether she is dead or alive. I am worried.'

'I can understand how difficult it is to endure an acute distress. But, you don't need to worry when I am with you. I will find her and the thief by doing everything that comes in my power,' Rex said. His sympathy had a gloss of fallaciousness.

'Listen, I have planned the naming ceremony of my daughter in the subsequent week. I would like to invite you to the event,' Alfred said, giving him an invitation card.

'Thanks for the honour, Mr Lanchester. After all, this will be the greatest event in the town,' Rex said. As he walked towards the door, Alfred Lanchester accompanied him.

'I am hoping that you will come quick with your definite results,' Alfred said.

Rex nodded and left in the chariot.

Alfred locked the door and gazed at Florence, who stood behind him. 'Why are you looking at me like that?'

'What are you up to?'

'I have done my best to overcome the problems.'

'Did he talk about Madeleine?'

'I can't pressurise him if he is not able to find her,' Alfred said. 'What do you think?'

Florence seemed to be in a different mood. She came closer, spreading her arms around him, and moving her lips she whispered into his ears, 'I think it's my bathing time, and you should do the honour of a husband.'

Alfred's eyes shone with excitement. 'I have already done with it.'

'But, you haven't done with the way I wanted.'

'What do you mean?'

'I am surprised. How can you forget the most important day of your life? Today is our anniversary.'

'Oh! I am sorry,' Alfred said. 'It seems you got something special today.'

Florence kissed him softly and said, 'It's a surprise.'

Alfred trailed her to the bathroom that had turned into a paradise. He gazed at the beauty around him as she had enriched it well with scented candles and flowers. The glasses of wine next to the bathtub were excellent complements to a royal bath.

The next minute, they went in the tub, exchanging flirty glances with each other.

'So this is what you have been fantasising about.' Alfred said.

Florence laughed. 'Well, you are good at reading my mind.'

'You are growing beautiful every day.' Alfred said.

'I thought I was ageing,' Florence said. 'How would you describe a beauty?'

'I am not a poet. I would rather say I have it all here.'

Florence was staring at him while she sipped some wine. 'How much you trust Rex Vabsley?'

'Someone usually believes others.'

Florence smiled. 'Do you think he is eligible for performing task he is holding?'

'Well, he is more than what you think he is capable of doing. He is going to find Madeleine and the thief. Madeleine knew where the key was hiding, and the thief who stole the box was aware of its secret.'

'So the thief believes that Madeleine knows everything about the key?'

Alfred nodded. 'I am very sure that her abductor will give one more try. But, this time, there will be no escape for him.'

Florence turned serious. 'This is getting worse. I don't know if he would keep her alive. What is there in abandoned castle?'

'It is empty. The guards have searched almost every ancient monument because those are the places where Carlton usually perform evil rituals.'

'If this is the case then it is virtually impossible to find Madeleine.'

'Let's hope for the best,' Alfred said, raising the glass of wine to his lips.

A few miles away, Carlton Stoker has visited Rex Vabley's house with an intention to have the key. He had granted him enough time to find it. Rex stood in silence for a moment. The imploding disappointment in his mind was remarkably noticeable on his face, and Carlton took no time to understand that he has not finished the task yet.

'So, you don't have the key.' Carlton said.

'It is not what you are thinking. You have no idea how much risk I have taken. How embarrassing you would feel if you were told to break into someone's home like a thief?' Rex asked.

'How did you know about the key?' Carlton asked.

'Madeleine had told me that the key was in the golden box. But, it wasn't there.' Rex replied with frustration.

Carlton had a big smile on his face. 'Madeleine! You can make her realise what you can do to her if she refuses to cooperate.'

'She is dead.'

'What?' Carlton's smile was disappearing into a shock.

'I have killed her,' Rex said.

'Hell with you, Mr Vabsley. You can't stand before me with those aggravating statements. You should have kept her alive,' Carlton said.

'What were you going to do with the key?' Rex asked.

'I would have released a ghost,' Carlton said.

There was silence for a moment. And then, Rex Vabsley laughed out loud. 'You want to do what?'

'This is not funny, Mr Vabsley.'

'What if I say I don't believe you?'

'In such cases, I always preserve the evidence.'

'Are you trying to convince me that ghosts do exist in this world?' Rex asked.

'Once, I was laughing like you are, Mr Vabsley. Since I ventured to learn the evil art of sorcery, I have been discovering mysteries of the invisible world.'

Rex Vabley's face turned serious. 'If you are so sure about your preserved evidence, Mr Stoker, then let's not waste any more time.'

Carlton nodded. 'Come with me, Mr Vabsley. I will show you the ghost.'

CHAPTER 6

Rex and Carlton travelled in a chariot to an isolated castle that was supposed to be the home of spirits. Hiding behind the door of a large chamber, Rex was now witnessing an incident that was beyond imagination. The ritual performers had lent the castle to the ghost for its gratification. It had seized a woman in his arms.

Today, the grey rocky walls revealed another secret of human contentment. The chamber reverberated with her joyous laughter and sensual whispers. Rex saw the woman on the bed, but not the ghost. The candles burning in the room drew two shadows on the wall of which one belonged to the woman and other to the unseen entity – the ghost.

'Look,' Carlton whispered, 'there is nobody with her on the bed. But there are two shadows on the wall having fornication.'

For the first time in life, Rex saw the ghost in the form of a shadow.

'This is unbelievable. Why is that woman indulged in lovemaking with a ghost?'

'Once, when her husband had a worst demonic possession, a few priests tried to relieve him from the deadly torment. The devil was none other than the woman's dead lover, who proved to be a strong contender for the holy rites, and he killed all the priests who were involved in an exorcism. Finally, the devil freed her husband after the woman's approval of his liaison with her.'

The world had been a house of mysteries; some of them were explored while others remained as the secrets. Today, Rex believed that ghosts do exist in the real world, and he sank deep in worriment after imagining the condition of Jeanette.

'I will find the golden key at the earliest, but before that take me to my wife,' Rex demanded.

Carlton took no time to fulfil his request. He blindfolded him before getting him into the chariot, not allowing him to read the path that leads to a secret place.

After an hour, Rex found himself alone standing between the grey walls. He was in a dark dungeon having several chambers connected to each other. At the corners, fire torches were fixed on the walls for some light. The ceiling had a leakage and the water drops falling on the ground were heard precisely. Rex started exploring the chambers, and finally, met Jeanette in one of them.

She was overwhelmed by his surprising appearance. She embraced him tightly with tears in her eyes. 'Rex, how did you get in?'

'Carlton brought me here.'

'He is still alive? I thought you killed him.'

'I wish I could, but my hands are tied.'

'Have you informed Alfred Lanchester about me?'

'No. If I do anything against Carlton's command, you will be dead in a moment.'

'Then, what are you going to do? I am scared.'

'Do you trust me?'

'Of course, I believe you.'

'Have they done anything wrong with you.'

'No.'

'Don't worry. I will get you out of here very soon.'

Just then, a guard entered the chamber and spoke, 'Your time is up.'

Rex looked into her eyes and kissed her as hard as he could. Then, he walked with the guard into the hall where Carlton shared a drink with him.

'Mr. Stoker, finding the key is impossible now. And I don't understand what treasure the ghost will bring to you.'

'I have no greed for treasures. All that I want is Alfred's death. He had been a curse to my family. His father had destroyed my family, and without taking his life I couldn't bring peace to their souls,' Carlton said.

'Mr. Stoker, you abducted my wife. You made me a thief. But, you never told me that you wanted to kill Alfred Lanchester. I can make your wish come true.'

'Well, I don't think so.'

'Alfred had invited me to his daughter's naming ceremony, and there will be a great party. All I have to do is alter his food or drink with poison,' Rex said.

'That is a good idea but I hope it works.'

'I give you my word. You will see his funeral very soon.'

Carlton didn't know if Rex Vabley's statement was a swindle or a new game plan. However, for saving the life of Jeanette, Rex has to kill Alfred by any means.

One week later, when the naming ceremony started in a ballroom, Rex Vabsley was seeking a chance to kill Alfred. It was during the dusk when the leaders along with their wives arrived from different towns. The enchanting music and the elegant ball dancers captivated the audience. Some couples among them were dancing while the others became spectators. The ambience of candle-lights dispersed equally, manifesting the beauty of costumes and the ballroom beyond comparison.

The guests were enjoying except Martina and Wilfred, who took a seat in the corner gazing at the event. After an unendurable agony, Martina had hardly left any tears to shed. She was thinking, how ill-fated one could be. After enormous efforts from all the guards, there was no sign of Madeleine as of now.

'Madeleine was waiting for this event desperately,' Martina said.

Wilfred grabbed her palm and said, 'I can understand you are going through a traumatic experience. I loved your sister more than myself. I can feel the way you are feeling now; the memories of our past are disquieting my mind as I am missing her so much. She was my first love, and I am still feeling that she is waiting for me at the lakeshore. I can feel the emptiness every moment.'

'I want to visit the lakeshore again. She must be waiting there,' Martina cried.

Wilfred knew that there was no point in haunting the lakeshore again. But, for her satisfaction, he agreed to go with her after the ceremony.

The hall was filled with enthusiasm when it was time to name the baby, and with the blessing of guests and a priest, the child was named as Carolina.

Right after hearing the name, Martina fell on knees and burst into tears in the memory of Madeleine, who had once suggested this name for the baby. The emotions were overflowing and Martina was losing control over herself.

The servants in the ballroom were serving drinks to the guests and Rex noticed that a servant had filled two trays, containing seven glasses of each. The servant picked the first one and walked to serve the guests.

Rex Vabsley seized this opportunity and altered one of the drinks with poison in the second tray.

A minute later, the servant came for the second one and moved towards the group of ministers. Rex Vabley's plan lacked perfection. He was hunting in the dark, and soon it seemed to fail.

Alfred was fortunate enough to pick a safe drink. Beside him, Alonso Mccrodden, a sixty-year-old minister picked the poisoned drink and hoisted the glass along with his companions. A few moments after emptying the glass, Alonso began to cough hard and fell on the floor and died.

Alonso's son, Van Mccrodden was worried and scared. He shook him and spoke, 'Father, wake up. What happened to you?'

Since there was no answer from Alonso, he realised that he was talking to dead. A trail of blood came out of his mouth and there was no pulse found in his heart or veins. He was surely dead.

Van Mccrodden burned with rage and held Alfred as the culprit.

A few years before, there was a war between Alfred and Alonso, and later, the things got better after the settlement and mutual understanding between them. Van Mccrodden believed that Alonso's murder was a planned one, and he declared war against Alfred Lanchester. Now, Blitzland was once again in danger as the army of San Mekenza was thrice than the military of entire Blitzland.

Alfred was not guilty as he knew he wasn't the actual culprit. Though his deprecation had a strong fortitude, the death of Alonso has proved to be disastrous to Blitzland. The guests have made an unceremonious departure after the unforeseen catastrophe. Last year when Alfred lost the battle, Florence was apprehensive over the imminent threat in consideration with his temperament for revenge and fury. This night, he was believed to be seeking vengeance for the loss in the battle, but the truth was quite different from what others were thinking.

Alfred walked into the bedroom where Florence sat with growing nervousness.

'Alfred, tell me you haven't done it,' Florence said.

'No, I have not. Don't you trust me?'

'I know you more than you know yourself. Just wanted to make sure that you are not seeking revenge, which is the foundation of war having no place for compromise, and that is making me worried.'

'If I ever wanted to take revenge,' Alfred said with annoyance, 'I would have declared a war instead of attacking Alonso like a coward. The culprit is undoubtedly one among the guests.'

'Perhaps, you are right. He might be the one who had abducted Madeleine.'

Florence was excellent at predictions and judgmental calls, but the perfection of ensnaring the actual culprit lacked behind. She could hardly comprehend her subordinator's cruel intentions, who had betrayed her deliberately. Surprisingly, Alfred Lanchester gave another task to Rex Vabsley to find the murderer of Alonso Mccrodden.

CHAPTER 7

Van Mccrodden was smart enough to play war tricks. He had declared war the next day, but he didn't attack. This incident ruffled rumours among the people that Van Mccrodden had withdrawn his declaration as he had boozed a lot in the party and was out of his consciousness last night. However, there was no evidence either that could prove the termination of the upcoming war. Alfred Lanchester secured the town with many soldiers, but a few days later he concluded the patrolling. People, mostly the women, felt safer now. They began to hang out and carry on their work.

Alfred wrote letters to Van, confessing for what had happened in the event, but none of them were responded.

A few weeks later –

Van with his army arrived in chariots and on horses, intending to annihilate the city of Blitzland. The soldiers scattered in all directions, entering the market and lanes between the houses, and with the flaming torches, they set the town on fire. However, the guards of Blitzland confronted the enemies with courage, which gave rise to a ferocious battle. Though Alfred Lanchester and his guards succeeded in lethal takedowns, Van Mccrodden was able to reach the palace where Florence and the baby stayed in the security. A few indoor guards confronted him, but they couldn't withstand his attack. The gunfire became a forewarning to Florence that she wasn't safe anymore, and along with her baby she escaped through a secret door.

Van's face turned red with rage and disappointment because of the absence of Florence. Undoubtedly, his brutal intention would have caused enough trouble for her if she had stayed there. However, she had found a chariot on the street to hide.

The scene on the street was terrifying and deadly. Injured townies fell upon the dead bodies those have already stained the streets with blood. Florence grasped her mouth as a deafening scream could have come out of it, but somehow she managed to take control over her fear.

The enemies were stabbing people with swords and a few of them were shooting them with rifles. Florence was witnessing the corpses lying in abundance after the enemy's atrocious crime on the street. They seemed to be brutal monsters in hats and boots, who were riding horses audaciously through the lanes to shed more blood.

Florence thought that the chariot was the safest place to hide until she felt a jerk and noticed that it had started moving. Unfortunately, the charioteer was a soldier of Van Mccrodden, who drove the chariot out of the city and reached no man's land; the region where there was no source of food or water.

It was during the dusk when Venus – the evening star blazed in splendour, dominating other astral bodies in the space. The sun has set, leaving a dull orange and pink hues in the west. Florence saw a comet travelling in the sky with a dusty trail leaving behind. She wished for the betterment of her life before the comet blazed bright for a moment and disappeared in the infinity. Her prayer had enough fortitude, but the baby cried loudly that drew the attention of the charioteer. He halted immediately to see who was hiding inside. He opened the door and gazed surprisingly at Florence and the baby.

'Mrs. Lanchester! What a surprise. Van Mccrodden is finding you, and you are hiding in my chariot. You should have at least confirmed to whom this chariot belong to. With all the efforts you took to run away from Van Mccrodden, you have put yourself in terrible predicaments like a fish is in the trap,' the charioteer said, locking the door from outside.

Florence was stunned, and she had no idea of what would happen next. The chariot was moving and there was no way to escape.

The moon had risen, and the lantern fastened to the chariot was undulating to and fro along with the motion. The mist revealed the wall and the entrance gate through which the chariot entered the city of San Mekenza; the place where Van Mcroddon was born and brought up. Moving in the alleys further, it came straight to the palace where Van's wife lived. Her name was Marcia Mcroddon – a young stunning beauty in an Edwardian gown. Her glamour had apparently enchanted every man residing in the city, and most of them fantasised of her being their wife. Tonight, her eyes were set on the street when the chariot entered the porch through a gate and stood in between a huge fountain and the front door. Like any other loving wife, her anticipation for Van was evident and overpowering, but the circumstances have changed. Van was missing. The soldier had no news regarding him, but he had a hostage instead.

'You have done a great job,' Marcia said. 'Lock her in the dungeon of an old castle, and tell Alfred to bring Van to me. I guess, Alfred has arrested him.'

The soldier followed the command and he took Florence and the baby to the dungeon.

The chances of Van's defeat was high despite his vast army as there was an inappropriate planning of attack. Marcia's plan was simple; exchange a life with a life, and she knew that Alfred would stop Van from attacking further, not by killing him but by proving himself on the part of the victory. He would try to snatch Van's weapon and convince him that he wasn't the murderer of Alonso.

Marcia's judgement had no connection with reality.

When Alfred Lanchester reached his palace after the demolition of enemies, he found the corpses of soldiers on the floor. Moreover, he didn't find Florence anywhere. He thought Van Mccrodden had abducted Florence.

Alfred rode his horse miles away to San Makenza. He rushed into Marcia's palace and met her.

'Where is my wife?' Alfred demanded.

'Where is my husband?' Marcia asked.

'I don't know where he had gone.'

'You didn't confront him in the war?'

'No. I don't even know if he was there.'

'Let me be more specific about this, Mr Lanchester, if you don't find Van, you will never find your wife.'

'Is this a new strategy to win the war?'

'Sorry, but I am already standing on the winning side.'

'If you were not a woman, I would have killed you.'

'Your words are annoying and useless. Let's see who wins,' Marcia said, throwing a sword at him while she chose one for herself.

The war between them started inside the palace, using the cover of candle stands, curtains, and furniture. At a certain point, Alfred lost the sword and fell near a table. Now, Marcia raised her sword to cut his skull, but Alfred pulled the drawer above him and saved himself. He quickly rolled over and grabbed the sword again.

The fight continued.

Finally, Marcia's sword broke away, and all that she was holding was a handle.

'You have bad weapons,' Alfred commented. He threw his sword and walked away.

After the worthless fight, Van Mccrodden was neither in the field nor in the palace. Then, where the hell he had gone? Finding Van Mccrodden had become mandatory to save Florence and the baby.

CHAPTER 8

The sun had baked enough when Alfred Lanchester had called Rex Vabsley for some help.

'Rex, I was waiting for you,' Alfred said. Rex was the right person who could find Van, Alfred thought. 'Marcia Mccrodden had made my wife a hostage, and she is asking me to bring Van to her. But, Van Mccrodden is missing. I need your help to find him.'

'Leave it up to me, Mr Lanchester. I will put all my efforts to fulfil her demand and save your wife.'

'How will you do it, Rex? And what if he is dead? We have to assume all the possibilities before we take any further step.' Alfred's point was valid, but he had no idea that the man whom he trusted the most had already betrayed him.

'I am sure he is not dead or else you would have found his body. You have searched every corner of the town, haven't you?'

'Of course, I have been looking for him since last night, but there is no evidence confirming his death.'

'I see. That means he is alive.'

'I have no idea where the hell he is hiding. He has disappeared like a ghost.'

'Don't worry Mr Lanchester; I will ask my soldiers to search him again. But, I don't understand how Marcia abducted Florence when she was not in Blitzland?' Rex was trying to figure out what would have happened during the war.

'This was Marcia's plan I guess, or why would she ask me to bring Van to her? She must have sent somebody to abduct Florence. However, all that matters to me is her safety. How can you be so sure that she wasn't in Blitzland?' Alfred's question seemed like a puzzle, but Rex was intelligent enough to solve it.

'It is very evident, Mr Lanchester, that she is not a fighter or a soldier. I have seen her in the naming ceremony and none of the guests spoke about her courage. Well, that is not my concern. All I need to do is, find Van Mccrodden.'

'I hope you would come up with some good news.'

Rex Vabsley nodded and left.

This late evening, Rex Vabsley reached San Mekenza to meet Marcia Mccrodden, who was playing piano in the large hall. After a long time, Rex was listening to the melodies of any instrument. He stood at the door watching her.

As soon as he caught her attention, she cringed.

Rex Vabsley, the subordinate of Alfred has entered my palace! He is the enemy.

'You take a step ahead, and you lose your head,' Marcia said, pointing a rifle at him.

'The world is full of mysteries and illusions. All that you see might not be true.'

Marcia sighed. 'I hate puzzles. Come to the point.'

'I am neither your enemy nor your friend. I am here to tell you something that you must know. Alfred has hidden a golden key in his palace. If you exchange Florence with the key and give it to me, I will do a favour to you.'

'What favour you are talking about?'

'Van Mccrodden is in my custody, and if you want to see him alive, you need to get the golden key.'

Dazed, Marcia moved the rifle down and spoke, 'So you were the game planner.'

'I wanted to kill Alfred in the ceremony, but Alonso Mccrodden mistakenly picked the wrong drink.'

'I need to send one more letter to Alfred Lanchester.'

'Hurry up; your husband is waiting for you.'

Tonight, Rex was holding the dice of the game and everything was going according to his plan. Marcia was in conformity with his demand, and she asked a soldier to deliver a letter to Alfred Lanchester.

After reading the letter from Marcia, Alfred went into a room and removed a mirror and grabbed the key from a small shelf in the wall.

Late at night, he reached no man's land in the chariot and waited for Marcia. Soon, she arrived in a chariot and proceeded further with Florence and the baby.

'What are you going to do with the key?' Alfred asked her as soon as she stood in front of him.

'That is not your concern. No more questions, just give me the key,' Marcia said.

Alfred didn't care about the key as much as he cared for his family. He handed over the key to her and left along with Florence and the baby.

The night was dark enough; misty and silent, filled with the agony of citizens, who have lost their families in the attack, and some of them were injured severely. Florence stood near the window gazing at the streets and the houses those were emitting smoke from the smokestacks.

'Alfred, is this the end of the war or the beginning? How much blood our people have to sacrifice? Florence questioned.

'I can see the storm coming for our lives. And this is certainly not the end.'

'Did she know the secret of the key?'

'No. The key was a sort of fortification to our family. If she wanted to kill us, then why did she release you?'

'Something is strange about Van. I didn't see him in the palace.'

'Van is missing. Marcia wanted me to take Van to her, but in the letter, it was clearly stated that she needed the key instead of him.

'This is strange. Why do you think the key became precious to her than her husband's life? Does it possess any other mystery?'

'I am not aware if it has a secret apart from the one I already know.'

'Look,' Florence said, 'not everything in life goes according to our wish. You lost the key, but you saved me.'

Alfred nodded.

A few hours before the dawn, Rex reached no man's land in the chariot where Marcia was waiting. He released Van from the chains.

'Give me the key,' Rex demanded.

Marcia threw the key at his foot.

Finally, after many efforts and risks, Rex Vabsley got the golden key.

Rex Vabsley reached his home and sighed in relief. That afternoon, he had a nap for a couple of hours.

In the evening, Carlton Stoker knocked his door and asked if he has got the key.

'Of course, Mr Stoker,' Rex said, 'I got the key. Please come in.'

Carlton walked a few steps and stopped. 'I am still wondering what made you reach for the key.'

'I didn't get to the key. It reached to me.'

'What have you done exactly?'

'Why you always want to know everything? Be happy with what you are having now.'

Carlton laughed. 'Ah! I am curious. Nevertheless, I must reward you for the completion of the task.'

Rex gave him the key and spoke, 'Hell with your rewards. I want my wife.'

'I am impressed,' Carlton said. 'Come with me; I will take you to your wife.'

It was raining late at night when they were travelling in the chariot.

'Where do you live? In the woods?' Rex asked.

'I live in the eyes of evil,' Carlton replied.

Rex smiled. 'Absolutely. I was expecting some stupid answer from you.'

'I live in the darkness where you met your wife a few days before. Evils love to live in the dark, you know.'

'I am sorry. I asked you a question. Please forgive me.' Rex felt the irritation right into his head.

Passing through the dark forest and the graveyard, they were now moving through the mountain path.

Rex peeped through the window and gazed at the castle that stood on the mountain peak. 'You kept her high.'

'That castle had been a part of history. People believed that the sorcerers in medieval era hung the sacrificed head on the door. Then, the spirits haunted it and spoke about their wishes.'

'Will you teach me the art of sorcery?'

'Not all the people pursue its knowledge as it requires special skills. I know you are not an ordinary person, but why you want to get into those creepy things?'

'Doesn't this question suits you better?'

'Yes, it does. My father was a sorcerer, who had passed the knowledge to my mother, and then it came to me.'

'So, she taught you to kill people.'

Carlton sighed and raised his palm and drew a finger over it. 'Everything is written here.'

'Palmistry! That is what you believe in.'

'Luck rules the life of humans. There is no achievement without it.'

'Efforts make the luck of a human, it doesn't come by birth,' Rex said, glancing at the castle that stood like a gigantic historical monument. 'We are almost there.'

The chariot stopped in front of the castle.

Carlton Stoker took him inside and pointed towards a chamber. 'Your wife is sitting in that room. Go and meet her,' he said.

Rex Vabsley opened the door and stayed motionless with his eyes stretched wide opened. He was staring at the corpse of his wife; bare and bathed in blood, hanging to the roof. The lightening that flashed on the dead gave a dreadful feeling. Now, turning towards Carlton, Rex was facing another grievous moment of fear. Carlton was standing behind him with a rifle.

'I told you Mr Vabsley; it's all about luck. Now you believe me? Your efforts are about to bring your death. Luck is everything, and I feel pity that your's isn't as good as mine.'

'You are the son of a bitch,' Rex said.

Those were his last words as the bullet cut his ribs and pushed him in the jaws of death.

This night was special for Carlton Stoker. He had not only fulfilled his dream but also brought some contentment to his dead mother's soul, just like the raindrops bring to the sun-parched land. Now, it was time to use the key. It was meant to unlock the door of a lighthouse at the seashore in the unsafe territory of man-hunters. They have frightened the people since they have randomly found anonymous heads in the woods by the shore. Man-hunters charged the travellers with their crossbows and daggers because of which they remained away from the region.

Despite the threat, Carlton Stoker never feared to haunt the area. He had once failed to break the door but succeeded to demolish a troop of man-eaters.

Tonight, Carlton moved on a horse and reached the woods near the beach. His curiosity grew to explore the region while he moved towards the lighthouse. Whenever Carlton explored the area, he escaped safely. But this time, it was something different. An arrow travelled in the air and penetrated straight into his bicep. He screeched and plucked it away and prepared to fire. There was a hunter hiding behind a tree and Carlton took no time to spot him and shoot him dead. He seemed to be one among the rare tribes, who have been residing in the forest.

In the next moment, Carlton found himself at the epicentre of their circular trap. Each of them had a crossbow pointing at him, and if they ever press the trigger, he would die instantly.

Carlton had prepared well for any circumstances. He did nothing and let them imprison him. The prison was a room in the house where they use to lock the victims. The tribes would dance by the fire before the dawn and then burn the victim to death. Later, they served the meat as an offering to God.

Among the tribal women, one unmarried stepped into the room with some food. She was a glamorous brunette. Two years before, an illicit fornication grew a cherishable relationship between them. Carlton sighed in relief as he knew she was the one to help him.

'I need your help,' Carlton said. 'There are dynamites in the saddle bag. I want you to bring them to me.'

'What are you going to do with them? I have a better idea instead,' she said.

She went out watching her friends arranging the woods for fire. When everybody left the spot to find more logs, she produced dynamites from the swaddle bag and placed them in the woods.

It was an hour before the dawn; the tribes began to dance as one of them ignited the woods. All the tribes gathered for fun. They played the drums and made creepy noises. Suddenly, the dynamites exploded, killing all of them.

The terrible woman now rushed into the room, but Carlton had already left on the horse.

After reaching the lighthouse, Carlton used the key to open its door and moved at its peak and found a gun in the glass. An antique gun that his father, Norman, had spelt with black magic was the weapon of destruction for Alfred's family. The gun was meant to break the unbreakable mirror that Seymour Lanchester had used for trapping the ghost during his wife's exorcism. The weapon was long and artistic, and the demolition of Alfred's family was certainly possible after releasing the spirit. Carlton Stoker made no delay to visit Gaston Fort – the fort where Seymour Lanchester had placed the mirror.

Carlton took almost a day to reach the fort.

The thunderstorm at night had turned worse than ever. Gaston fort looked scary like any other haunted monument in the flashy lightening. The dark walls seemed to have buried many mysteries among which one was revealing tonight. Carlton advanced into the fort and gazed at the walls. He removed a dirty cloth that was covering the mirror. It seemed as if the cloth had never protected the mirror from dust. It was so dull that even after standing in front of it, he could hardly see his reflection. He stepped close to the mirror and wiped off the dust with his palm. Just then, the scary ghost of a lady stared at him and he recoiled in terror.

Carlton Stoker had never imagined that he could see the ghost so effortlessly.

'Free me, I won't harm you,' the ghost whispered.

Carlton raised the gun and shot the mirror, releasing the spirit out into the world.

The lightening flashed dramatically on the castle and the surrounding while the ghost laughed out loud in a weird manner.

CHAPTER 9

That night, when the entire city of San Mekenza got drenched in the rain and went silent, Marcia Mccrodden grabbed Van in her arms as she slept on the bed in lingerie. The rainy weather has inspired them to celebrate the rare romantic moments with overflowing lustful fantasies. Tonight, it was proven that Marcia was wild and dominant as compared to Van in the matter of compassion and spirit. While she was indulged in lovemaking with him, she perceived a horrible image on the window. Marcia didn't know about it and she had never seen it before. It was the scary face of the ghost. Marcia recoiled with a deafening scream and she fell on the floor.

'Are you okay?' Van was trying to figure out what had happened to her. He turned around and scanned the room.

'I saw a face in the window,' she said.

Van marched towards the window, and suddenly the glass shattered and penetrated into his face and throat. He died instantly. Everything happened so fast that he didn't get time to save himself. Several seconds later, the floor was flooding with his blood.

Draped in the blanket, Marcia rushed out of the room. The invisible ghost blew away the candles, allowing the darkness to swallow the entire palace.

Scared and shivering, Marcia moved into the piano room locking the door behind her. Gasping heavily, she stepped backwards, her eyes still fixed on the door. The darkness aroused an overwhelming feeling of fear and anxiety in her.

Now, the ghost began to play the instrument and its sound echoed in the room. She had never ever faced such a fearful moment in her life. She tried to open the door, which barely moved an inch. Her eyes began to scan the dark room, and in the flash of the lightening, the ghost appeared right in front of her; enormously dreadful and weird.

Marcia felt like a shock travelling from her toe towards her head, and in a few moments, she fainted on the floor.

When the night passed away, Marcia awoke with the first streak of daylight. Draped in the blanket, she carefully stepped into the bedroom to see Van. He was on the floor, completely ruined and lifeless. Marcia's eyes were filled with tears of agony and pain.

That day after the funeral, Marcia walked on the muddy ground of the cemetery. Somewhat wet, she got into the chariot and leant forward, resting her elbows on her thighs, covering her face in the palms, she cried for one more time.

She remembered the way he proposed her – gifted her roses – kissed her for the first time – and spent first marriage night with her. The way he caressed her – moved fingers over her cheeks – smelled the perfume of her bosom – and the way he used to grab her in his arms. Whenever she played the piano, he would embrace her from behind in a loving manner. In the frosty mornings, they shared breakfast, accompanied each other during the bath, and played in the warm water. Marcia remembered every moment she had spent with him. The thought in which her mind was immersed has washed out the grief for a few moments, and then, the scary face of the ghost flashed in a trice.

The day was cloudy enough. Marcia asked the charioteer to stop as she passed by the lakeshore. She saw Alfred Lanchester and his guards, who were engaged in finding Madeleine. At least they thought of searching for something that would give them a clue where she had been hiding.

Marcia reached him. 'Mr. Lanchester, I am here to apologise for everything. For every misunderstanding, that stood between our friendship. My husband shouldn't have attacked Blitzland.'

Alfred nodded and smiled softly. 'You know what Marcia? Tears have the power to wash away all the sins. When you regret every mistake from the bottom of your heart, you become a wise human and a pure soul.'

Marcia had never thought that Alfred would be so kind towards her, though, he had lost his army, people, and peace. She felt a sudden relief from the guilt after listening to his words of sympathy. 'You are a man with a great heart who know that forgiveness is greater than punishment. I wish my husband would have understood this.'

'Did you find your husband?'

'He is dead. The ghost attacked him last night.'

Now, this news was more than a shock to Alfred Lanchester. He looked at her curiously. 'What have you done with the key?'

'I gave it to your subordinate, Rex Vabsley. He betrayed you. He made my husband a hostage and asked me to get the key from you.'

'Why would Rex betray me? He always intended to kill Carlton Stoker.'

'Rex might be the culprit, but I am equally responsible for hiding the truth,' Marcia said. She was still solving the puzzle in her mind. 'What do you know about the key?'

'Carlton Stoker needed the key because he wanted to release a ghost. Once that spirit had tried to kill my mother. I don't know if Rex was aware of it.'

'Time has changed everything. You never know what is going to happen ahead. I guess, Rex must be working for Carlton.'

Alfred gasped a deep breath and said passionately, 'I have to find him.'

Alfred Lanchester left in a chariot and reached the front porch of a Cathedral where he met a priest called William. Like any other priest he believed in God and the evils, and for the spiritual contentment of his soul, he wore a cross around his neck.

'Father,' Alfred said, stopping him in the lawn outside the Cathedral, 'I am in trouble, I need your help.'

'Mr. Lanchester!' William was surprised as he didn't expect him early this morning. 'What can I do for you?'

'Father, do you know why Gaston fort was abandoned?'

'Of course. Your father and I were best friends, and we shared every secret with each other.'

'If you know everything,' Alfred spoke with deep voice, 'then this news will terrify you.' Alfred sighed while he was looking into his eyes. 'Carlton Stoker has released the ghost.'

William glanced at the rainy clouds and moved the cross to his forehead, lips, and finally, to the chest. 'It is imperative for me to know what kind of ghost it is. Just like humans are divided into different races and religions, ghosts are categorised according to the way their bodies have died.'

'You mean, the ghosts have races too.'

'Yes. The theories say that if a woman dies as a virgin, her spirit haunts men to satisfy her lust. The death of a pregnant woman is considered as a curse for the children. In this case, the ghost hypnotises the children to take them away from their parents. There are many unproven theories about the spirit. Mr Lanchester, do you possess any object that belongs it?'

'Not really. But, what if I had one?'

'Seizing any haunted objects may risk your life. Most of the times, ghost follow the person who possesses things relating to it, either by devotedness or by physical connection.'

'That is strange. How far I can keep the evil away from my family, Father?'

'I know a ritual that can help us controlling the ghost, which is hard but not impossible,' William said. His theories based on demonic possessions and ghost-calling rituals have become prevalent in the last decade and helped many people to come out of the evil sufferings. 'Nobody in this world has escaped from the fate of death, and not every individual becomes a ghost until that person has desires to live with. Have you committed a sin?'

Alfred's face turned serious. 'No.'

'Pardon me, Mr Lanchester, but it seems as if your father had a purpose behind seizing the ghost.'

'Your point is valid. My father captured the spirit because it was the only way to save my mother during the exorcism.'

'But why did the ghost haunt your mother?'

There was a momentary silence as the cold breeze passed by them.

'I don't know,' Alfred replied. 'All I know is that the key was meant to fortify my family from the eyes of the evil.'

'To my knowledge, your father and Carlton's mother were enemies. Apart from being magicians, both were skilled witchcraft performers. Your father had stolen the key from Carlton's mother because she had prepared a gun that would break the mirror. The location of the weapon was a secret, and I am sure Carlton knew about it.'

'Is there any way to get rid of the ghost?'

William nodded. 'Take me to your palace. I will try my best.'

About an hour later, they were in the palace. After hanging a cross on the wall, William closed his eyes, praying for the betterment of Alfred's family.

May evil be destroyed and the world dwell in peace.

'This cross will protect your family. Keep praying for blessings every morning and your sins will be forgiven,' William said.

'Thank you, Father,' Alfred said.

'I have to go now. May God bless you,' William said.

CHAPTER 10

Late in the evening, Alfred stood near the window in the candle-lights, his mind equipped with perplexing questions regarding Madeleine. A couple of weeks have passed; yet, none of his guards were able to find her. He was unanswerable to her parents and relatives, who inquired about her day and night.

Martina, the servant, stood behind him and spoke, 'Mr. Lanchester, the dinner is ready.'

A minute later, Alfred joined Florence for the dinner.

'It is going to be a difficult situation if we don't find Madeline soon. Her family members have faith in me and I don't want to disappoint them,' Alfred said.

'What if she is dead?' Florence questioned in a serious tone. It was a genuine question, though, there were no shreds of evidence found that could prove her death.

'Rex Vabsley knows where she is, but he is not on our side anymore. He must have left Blitzland by now.'

'Do you remember I have asked you a question on our anniversary?'

'Yes. I remember. I shouldn't have trusted him.'

'From all the incidents and clues, I believe that Rex is not only an abductor of Madeleine but also a thief who tried to steal the key. He is also a murderer of Alonso Mccrodden. He spoiled our baby's naming ceremony,' Florence said. This time, she has spoken the fact.

'I wish Van Mccrodden would have kept some patience until the truth was revealed.'

Florence had taken a pause before she spoke, 'Van! He deserved the punishment. Our town is living a gloomy life after the war. At least he should have used his brain.'

'I received an apology from Marcia.'

'And you excepted it, despite knowing that she could have killed me.'

'I don't hate Van as much as I love my family,' Alfred said. 'You know what Florence? If immoral people cannot stop being bad for good, then why should genuine people cease to be good for bad?'

'I don't know what are you up to? But I am sure your philosophy is going to kill all of us one day,' Florence said. It seemed as if she had a different opinion.

A minute later, they heard two women screaming outside.

'My God! What is that?' Martina said, hurrying to the window. 'Mr. Lanchester, something is wrong there.'

Alfred got up, wiped off his fingers on a napkin, and said, 'You stay here.'

Alfred stepped out in the dark with an oil lamp and saw two women near a tree gazing at the deads. They were hanging upside down to the barks. At first, he didn't identify the bodies, since he was standing at a safe distance. As he tread further curiously, he drew the light on those two bodies and stood with his eyes wide opened. Surely, he knew them very well. They were none other than Rex and Jonette.

'Guards,' Alfred shouted.

They came running with spheres in their hands. 'Yes, sir.'

'Take these bodies to the palace. I want to have a close look.'

The guards placed bodies in the coffins and moved in the palace.

Martina stood in shock, staring at them. Her emotions flooded instantly after seeing Rex. She slapped him and yelled, 'You scoundrel, tell me where is my sister?'

Florence dragged her away while she cried. 'Martina, don't be stupid. We will find your sister.'

'How?' Martina questioned. 'He was the one who had her information.'

Florence was speechless. She threw a glance at Alfred.

He nodded.

Florence took Martina to her room.

Alfred Lanchester examined the bodies minutely, checked their pockets, but didn't find anything.

The next morning when the city was hiding in the mist, Alfred, Florence, and Martina reached the graveyard along with guards and a priest. When funeral got over, Martina gazed around and spotted a piece of cloth, partly coming out from the soil. She recognised to whom it belonged to. 'Madeleine,' she screamed. 'This is her dress.'

Naturally, the erosion of soil due to rain had revealed the mystery buried in it. They dug the spot and found her body.

The remorse gripped Martina's soul instantly and she cried constantly.

Madeleine's soul had already rolled into the arms of God. There was no sorrow, no fear, just a peaceful contentment, and liberation from all the botherations.

Though Madeleine had died in early ages, though she couldn't live the life she was blessed with, she lived in the heart of people forever. The sin-stained souls were subject to God's relentless punishment. It seemed as if forgiveness was never meant for them. They were punished for every pain they gave. For every tear, they brought into the eyes of the wise. After every battle of life, justice remained in the possession of wise, and there was no escape for the sinister.

That day, Madeleine's funeral was held in the presence of her loved ones. Wilfred, Martina, and rest of her family wept millions of tears in her memory. Life didn't seem the way they expected to be. Though her mortal body disappeared in the grave, her immortal love always remained in their souls.

Finally, with all the memories and tears, the day came to an end.

Since the sun has set, the darkness ruled over the town with the growing mist. Alfred Lanchester heard a strong fist on the door. First, second, and the third time till the guards opened it. It was William, striding inside the palace.

'Father, what's the matter?' Alfred asked, walking through the hallway.

The apprehension was intense as Willian gasped serval breaths and spoke, 'I saw the ghost of a woman,' he said. 'She looks horrible. She was asking me to remove the cross from your house.'

'Are you going to do it?' Alfred asked.

'Never,' William said. 'The cross is protecting your family.'

'But if you don't remove the cross, she will kill you,' Alfred said. His judgement was accurate this time. The ghost was intending to kill Alfred, but the cross was an obstacle in its way. Without wasting a minute, Alfred removed the cross from the wall and gave it to him. 'Father, please listen to me. Take the cross with you and bring your wife and grandson here in the palace. We will make a plan to trap the ghost, just like my father did.'

William nodded and moved out like a spiritual warrior, holding a weapon in one of his hands: the cross!

William's grandson, Peter, an eight-year-old boy, was mystified by her granny's behaviour. He stood in the bedroom behind her. Granny was on her knees, facing towards the wall. She giggled.

As Peter moved further, he gazed upon her long wavy hair and asked, 'Granny, can you get me some more milk?'

Peter raised the empty glass. The fierceness was exhibited in granny's eyes as she stood and gazed at him. Peter could feel her aberrant behaviour; since a day has passed, granny hasn't spoken a word. She replenished the glass with milk and gave it to him. Several seconds later, Peter sensed atypical taste as the milk had turned into the blood that rolled over his lips. Remarkably terrified, Peter dropped the glass and gazed at his granny.

She asked him if he wants some more.

When she spoke, a mixture of two ponderous voices was heard, and the absence of eyeballs in her eyes made her look scary. And then, fear and death ruled over.

A few minutes later, William entered the house and busted in tears after finding his wife and grandson lying dead on the floor.

People during that era would describe the ghost as an astral body with feelings but no brain. That's why the haunted women would shake their head abruptly with long hair, and climb the tree like a cat. They laughed like a giant and swing on the ropes at midnight. They loved to eat animals and humans, and many times they played with the skulls like a ball.

How it felt when the ghost haunted a person?

The person would feel a sudden weight on the body. Fainting suddenly and waking up with no eyeballs was the common symptom of a haunted person. The concept of haunting seemed scary in itself and it had threatened the entire city.

CHAPTER 11

The ghost has punished William for protecting Alfred, and despite losing his family, he continued reading chapters from Bible in the palace.

May God protect Alfred and his family and look upon him with mercy. May He destroy the evil and let the wise dwell in peace.

Even though William prayed from the bottom of his heart, not all the sins deserved forgiveness. The sinister were supposed to pay the debt of their sins to receive blessings from God. But then, there was one more precious thing that God expected from devotees – a strong faith in Him.

With the faith as vast as the ocean, William placed the cross on the wall and prayed again. His determination in the prayer kept him before God for more than an hour.

After the prayer had ended, Alfred came to William with a word of sympathy. 'Father, I am sorry,' he said. 'I have troubled you a lot. I am responsible for your family's death.'

William didn't understand why Alfred was regretting and holding himself responsible for the life-afflicting agony. Practically, William had nothing to do with his apology. "Apology" remained a word that only lived a moment, and then, there was a complete silence till William voiced his opinion.

'Stop blaming yourself,' William said. He walked to the window, gazed at the sky, and crossed his hands behind him. 'You can neither have control over death nor the destiny. My agony was written in this way.'

William's statement has surprised Alfred. It needed a lot of courage to face the terrible moments of death, no matter if it comes to one among the family members, or swallow the entire family. Anyone would have appreciated his ability to understand the phenomenon of life including his endurance to withstand hardship. Being a true believer of God, he well understood the law of nature.

One was born to die.

Death was not a curse, but a boon.

Could anybody imagine life without death? An unending journey with whatever one has got? Why have people been enjoying every spark of the new sun? Or the changing seasons? Everybody needed a change. Only Change could modify the universe and nothing else.

Change – the rule of nature lasted forever.

Though Alfred's heart was filled with veneration for William and his knowledge, he raised a question that was an undeniable fact. 'Aren't humans the sculptors of their lives?'

'Yes, they are! But, not all the time.'

According to William, a person's efforts cannot be fruitful unless he had a good fortune running. But, what about the ghost? Does anybody's luck say that the ghost would be the reason for death?

It seemed as if Alfred didn't want to get deep into philosophy. All he wanted is to trap the ghost or send it in the universe so that it would never return again. 'What should we do now? Is there any way to get rid of the ghost?'

William had found out a method of liberating the spirit from this world. He had learned it from his ancestors. It was some ritual that required two men and two women, who would sit in opposite direction, holding their hands together to form a circle. The invisible ghost shall be invited in the circle and then liberated.

What was the risk in the process?

Anybody who opened eyes before the completion of the process would die.

Alfred Lanchester wrote a letter and sent his guard to receive Marcia Mccroddon. This opportunity would redeem her mistake. Complying with the demands, Marcia made no delay to reach the palace.

Though they were ready for the ritual, one question stood significantly in front of them: who will take care of the baby? Soon, they found the answer.

Madeleine's sister, Martina. She took the baby to the orphanage where she had spent initial years of her life. Tonight, she met a lady caretaker, who told her that the institution had closed years before. Somehow she convinced the custodian by telling her that she worked in the minister's palace. Then, she left her in a room. The old furniture and rotten walls clearly defined that the building was at least a hundred-year-old. However, she managed to stay there for a day.

When the night fell with mysterious darkness, she lighted a few candles in the room. A mirror on the wall became the scariest part when she witnessed a horrible image of the ghost, who stood beside the baby with a knife. Martina turned, but the ghost had vanished, not forever, but maybe for a few moments. The dread was eating her mind little by little. Now, in spite of receiving a warning from the ghost, only a fool would stay there. Moreover, there was no point in communicating with the caretaker as she would never see it.

At the other hand, Alfred, Florence, William, and Marcia prepared themselves for the ritual. Before starting the process, William gave them the instructions.

Nobody shall open the mouth, eyes, or leave the hand or pay attention to the voices and things appearing around.

Never respond to any question or turn back if anybody calls the name.

The ghost would try different ways to deflect their mind, but they have to remain calm.

Ghosts have the ability to recognise the state of mind. They target the people who lack the strength of mind. They tend to frighten the people with their scary appearance.

A minute later, they sat on the floor and gripped each other's hands. William asked them to close their eyes before he started to whisper a few spells, and then, went quiet. There was a pin drop silence that lasted for a few moments. Then, the ghost made a scary noise, which sounded like a factory siren.

The windows shattered into pieces. The paintings left the wall and fluttered in the air. The scene looked extremely horrible, even for any courageous person on the earth. And how would an ordinary person behave in this frightening situation? The answer was obvious. *He would die in horror.*

Though there was no limit to fear, Martina had entered the palace with the baby and tried to grab everybody's attention. She screamed from the bottom of the heart. 'Open your eyes, please. She is coming for us. She will take away the baby.'

The soul of a mother was trembling with fear. She couldn't even imagine of losing the baby in her dream. The baby was at risk, but William had already told her that the ghost would play tricks to divert her mind, due to which Florence remained calm and didn't open her eyes.

'Oh my God! She is coming,' Martina screamed again.

Now, the baby was crying as bad as the soul of its mother. Florence hardly tolerated the growing threat and the fear of losing her child. The worriment had frozen her face, and her eyes went pale. Yes, she had opened them.

Moving quickly to Martina, she grabbed the baby in her arms and gazed at it with love and affection. She looked up to thank Martina, but she had already disappeared.

Now, the real Martina strode into the hall with the baby, confusing Florence of what she was holding. She looked into the face of the child that was a ghost with no eyes, but the holes as dark as the dread that penetrated deep into her soul. Florence screamed out loud, and her nose, eyes, ears began to bleed, and the baby turned into ashes.

Alfred and Marcia tried to help her, but her head left the body and rolled on the floor and cracked like a parched land after the earthquake.

Kneeling down near her headless body, Alfred wailed in pain.

CHAPTER 12

The next day has risen.

Florence's death has seized Martina with unusual craziness. She broke all the mirrors in the palace and didn't allow anyone to come closer to her. She believed that the ghost resided in the palace, in the objects, inside the mirrors. Alfred tried to convince her that the devil had gone far away and would never return.

When Marcia went clam in the chair, William took Alfred away from her to have a word with him. 'This is not the way it should happen. We need to do something to stop the entity. Maybe, we need one more person who has a strong mind power to control the ghost. You see, it is all about courage.'

'Oh God! This job is going to take too long. How am I suppose to know the right person with enough guts? Can you please tell me, Father, how do you measure the courage?'

'Mr. Lanchester, I can understand your situation. Courage cannot be measured, but a person can be judged who has it enough. We have to find someone having extraordinary sense.'

Alfred Lanchester sat in the chair with disappointment. He had no idea about any particular person. Alfred thought for a while and stood with anticipation. 'Father, I know a person who may help us. Her name is Loretta Costigan. She is blind, but she can see the future. She has an extraordinary sense.'

'Are you sure she is the right person?'

'Yes. She was the one to tell me about her nightmare, the destruction she had seen. In her opinion, something wrong was going to happen after the birth of the baby. And see, her dream had turned into reality. At first, Van Mccrodden attacked Blitzland. Then, the ghost was released. And now, I lost my wife. According to her prediction, nothing went right after the baby's birth.'

Now, William had a slight smile on his face. He saw a spark of hope in the dark. 'Mr. Lanchester, if you know her very well, then let's bring her in the process.'

Alfred and William went to meet Loretta Costigan in a chariot, and an hour later, they were sitting in front of her parents. The spark of hope was vanishing when her mother, Edyth, refused for lending her daughter to them. 'You want my daughter to deal with the ghost so that she can die like your wife, Mr. Lanchester?'

'If she doesn't help us, we all have to die,' Alfred replied.

'Well, I don't think so,' Edyth replied. 'To my knowledge, the ghost want to kill you and not my daughter.'

'Mrs. Costigan, you have no idea how badly we have been through this misery. I admit, the ghost has haunted my family, but it doesn't mean that it is not going to haunt yours. Who knows what will happen in the future?' Alfred said.

'The ghost is becoming aggressive day after day, and if we don't stop it, it might kill the entire town,' William said. It seemed as if Edyth didn't assimilate his non-evident judgement. Whereas, Jean Costigan, neither believed in the existence of God nor the evil. This scepticism in religious theories made him a reluctant soul in the spiritual world. He was hearing the conversation that left no impact on him. However, he had never permitted Loretta to talk about the nightmare to anyone, but his wonderment lied in the fact that Alfred had faith in her dream.

'If you don't believe us, then ask your daughter. She has seen the annihilation of Blitzland,' Alfred said.

'Loretta's opinion is as significant as my approval. You must have a word with her before proceeding further,' Edyth said.

Bessie brought Loretta to voice her opinion. Loretta had been waiting to solve the mystery of her nightmare. Since her childhood, she had believed in the phenomenon of nature – there was always a boon after a curse, and the boon behind the blindness was her extra sense.

'Till now, the people have shown their sympathy towards me. They have helped whenever I was in need. Now, it is my turn to redeem their favour,' she said.

Edyth's keenness to comprehend her daughter's role in the ritual was quite significant as far as she knew that none of these customs were free from life-wrenching disasters. Concerning her plea, William explained to her that Loretta has to enter into the unconsciousness state of mind and help the ghost to reach the spiritual light.

Though Loretta was a child at heart, haunting had been a strange part of her life. The dreams have been haunting her since she was born, but tonight, she was going to haunt the dreams.

The night has arrived with a thrashing thunderstorm. Loretta laid on the floor, concentrating on every breath as one would do in meditation. She felt weightless as the extraordinary sense took her spirit into the timeless world during the process. Emerging from the dark, a beam of light drew her attention, and she travelled towards it till it grew intense and finally vanished, bringing her into the previous life.

CHAPTER 13

Tonight, the town seemed to be wrecked in a ferocious battle between wise and imprudent. The houses were on fire, and souls of dead were burning in flames of revenge. The screams of townies shattered the peace of the night when enemies battered them mercilessly. Some of them were razed with fathomless haemorrhage and perished instantly. It all seemed like an epic war without imparting any justification for its cause. The defenders drew out the possibility that the antagonists might have meticulously executed evil's command since many of them worshipped evil to acquire powers and possessions. Their acquisitiveness turned rampant, and none of the properties satisfied them.

Evils were the people who efficiently performed depraved rituals, including human sacrifice and naked blood-bath. Their greediness like the waxing moon grew to inspire them to rob and slaughter the townies and shed the blood as an affectionate tribute to the evil. The blood was streaming through the streets, proving to the God of evil that they have done immeasurable ferocious murders, and they believed that evil would give them what they desired.

Loretta Costigan, holding her attractive Edwardian dress above her ankles ran barefoot through a narrow lane. She was the only one to survive the attack without acute lacerations. She was fair-skinned; her hair bound in a bow, and her eyes were dark emerald; alluring but terrorised after having perceived the deadly war. The tiny stones on the streets have bruised her feet, but that pain was incomparable to what others were enduring. A few people wrapped in the flames ran on the street with their hands in the air. They were screaming as if thousands of knives ran through their skin at a time. Loretta had never seen anything like this before; people on flames alive! She looked minutely through a slight crease between the houses and gazed upon a few kids who were frozen with fear; some cried while others stood with their eyes fixed at the horrifying scene: The enemies frightening and murdering people with flintlock rifles.

Loretta Costigan scampered through the winding path in the dense woods. Being swallowed by the growing mist, she halted on the lonely street; gasping and sweating. As she suspiciously trod further, the mist faded away revealing a massive gate of the garden that was meant for lovers. The entrance of garden had its name painted on a curved log: Morgane's Park.

Tonight, there were no lovers, no families, but a mother along with a baby knelt in front of two formidable enemies. She was begging for her life.

Despite the swelling effulgence of rising moon, Loretta barely saw their faces while she stood motionless, witnessing a heinous crime being committed.

'I beg your kindness. Please don't shoot me, I have a child,' the mother said, glancing at them anxiously with drenched eyes. She thought at least those monsters would show humanity and leave her, but the situation turned worse beyond imagination.

'I won't shoot if you admit to being my servant for rest of your life,' a soldier said.

'No, that is impossible. Please let me go,' the woman replied.

The woman's eyes appeared in tears; even so, filled with fear and anger at the same time. The gunmen were monsters with no mercy in their heart. They raised their weapon and shot her dead.

Now, Loretta witnessed this brutal murder. But this time, she didn't sprint towards the chariot. She advanced further to see the faces of the culprits. They were none other than Van Mccrodden and Alfred Lanchester! They had committed a sin in their previous life, and the ghost of the dead mother haunted them in the present to avenge her death. Now, the dead mother had awoken. She stared at her with the deepest resentment. 'Leave me alone,' she said.

'I am here to liberate you. I will take you to the spiritual light. Come with me,' Loretta said.

The ghost was annoyed, and it looked straight into her eyes those became a victim of her vehemence. As a result, they began to bleed.

Loretta screamed out loud, coming back to consciousness, her eyes were now bleeding for real. Alfred and William were worried as they would be responsible if anything wrong have had happened to her. Loretta was all right. Then, she explained to them how Alfred's life-past sin was carried into this life. It was yet another fairytale.

Loretta had seen the past and not the future. She was apprehensive for the baby's safety as the ghost with the evil power would seek complete avenge. There was one person who could liberate the spirit effortlessly. And that person was none other than Carlton Stoker.

Now it was imperative to seize Carlton Stoker for freeing the spirit. They have to kill his guards and get into the graveyard castle where he performed sorcery. They loaded their flintlock pistols and rifles.

'Mr. Lanchester,' Martina said, entering the room. 'It's my right to avenge my sister's death. I am going along with you.'

'Who will take care of the baby?' Alfred asked.

Marcia Mccrodden was standing at the door, listening to the conversation. She interfered, 'Mr. Lanchester, let her go with you. I will take care of the baby.'

Alfred nodded and gave a rifle to Martina. Then, he went to William and asked him to grab a weapon.

'I am the first priest in the world to grab a gun instead of the cross,' William said. He chose a flintlock pistol.

They moved in a chariot through the bouncy bridle path, then the forest, and finally the graveyard. There was a momentary appearance of the ghost in the woods that shook their mind with terror as they knew very well that their weapons were not meant for any supernatural forces.

The sun was about to set when they hide in the castle, anticipating Carlton, who usually performed evil rituals after the dusk. If anyone had been enumerating the sacrificed people, then tonight it would be the hundredth one. Since human sacrifice was the only way of possessing evil powers, Carlton did what he was supposed to do.

On his command, the guards dragged a victim in the castle, who was a beautiful woman like every man would dream about. She was about to go through a dark torment before sacrificing her life, maybe, the guards intended to violate her, and Alfred didn't want that to happen. He gestured William and Martina to shoot his guards, but not Carlton, as he would need him to liberate the ghost. As soon as the firing started, the guards took position and return-fired. The chaos lasted for ten minutes, and then there was a complete silence. Fortunately, Alfred and his companions took control over Carlton and made him sit on a chair. They received a few words of gratitude from the lady for saving her life. She looked into the eyes of Carlton, slapped him right on his face, sighed a deep breath, and walked away.

Carlton Stoker was on the point of a rifle. He had no option besides adhering to their commands which were entirely visible to him. He was supposed to liberate the ghost by using the art of sorcery.

Carlton sat on the floor where the star was drawn. A few candles were burning in it, and the book of witchcraft was lying on the stand. The book had all the ways to deal with astral powers. Flipping the pages, he went on reading the spells until the candles blew away, signalising the arrival of the ghost.

Carlton started emitting fumes from his ears, nose, and mouth. He wailed in pain. 'She doesn't want to go.'

The fumes revealed the blood, spreading all over the floor and brought Carlton to death. He had lost his life right in the middle of the ritual, and there was no way to get rid of the spirit.

'This is not a safe place anymore. Let's go to the palace,' Martina said.

When they reached the palace, William came up with one way that might help them in an exigency. 'Mr. Lanchester,' he spoke, 'you must leave the town right now. Maybe, you can save yourself.'

'What are you going to do?' asked Alfred.

'I am going to read Bible.'

'Where will you go, Mr. Lanchester?' Martina questioned.

Alfred went silent, but Marcia spoke, 'I am taking him to San Makenza.'

A few hours later, Alfred and Marcia along with the baby reached the palace.

'Do you think we are safe here?' Alfred asked, following her in the hall.

'In my opinion, this is the safest place in the world,' Marcia replied.

'Marica, I want to ask you something,' Alfred said, walking closer with a serious thought in his mind, which seemed to be overflown by emotions. 'Florence's death had left me completely alone in this miserable world. But, your presence in my life can fill up the gap forever. I know it's hard to accept me, but the truth is, I need a partner and my daughter needs a mother.'

Marcia nodded. 'Let's start a new life together.'

Alfred Lanchester felt relieved. He was overjoyed and decided to marry her soon, maybe the next day. What stood between them was one stormy night that came with deafening thunders and lightening.

At the other hand, William and Martina had finished reading the Bible in the palace. They were now hearing to the whimpering sounds coming from the dark chamber. They stepped into it with candles and discovered that those sounds were coming from a wardrobe. Slowly and carefully, they opened the wardrobe and found Marcia Mccrodden lying inside it with her hands, legs, and mouth tied with handkerchiefs. As soon as they relieved her, she spoke, 'I am the real one. She made me unconscious with her scary eyes. Did you let them go?'

At that moment, William felt like an earthquake. 'We have to hurry,' he screamed, rushing to the chariot.

In San Mekenza, the baby was sleeping between Alfred and Marcia. Soon, they heard someone knocking the door. Alfred walked slowly with suspicion and opened the door. Then, the shock pricked through his veins from head to toe. Marcia was standing in front of him with William and Martina.

'Where is she?' Marcia said with tears in her eyes.

They all rushed into the bedroom. The ghost had vanished along with the baby, and the bed was stained with blood, lot of blood.

Alfred knelt on the floor, crying and screaming. 'Kill me you bitch. Kill me.'

The dead mother had finally completed her revenge. Alfred's sin in his past life was unforgiving, and he was now paying the debt for it, not by dying at once, but for every moment throughout his life.

The ghost of the dead mother felt the contentment, and it never showed up again. It moved on through the graves and finally disappeared in the mist.

THE END

Printed in the United States
By Bookmasters